UNCOVERED UNDERCOVER

There was a flurry of shocked gasps and curses as everyone backed quickly away from Hawk, except for Fisher who stayed at his side. "You're the impostor!" cried the accusing MacNeil, drawing his blade.

There was a roar of outrage as the MacNeil led the others in pursuit. Hawk drew his own sword, but without his axe he didn't like the odds at all . . .

Ace Books by Simon R. Green

HAWK & FISHER
WINNER TAKES ALL
THE GOD KILLER
WOLF IN THE FOLD

GUARD AGAINST DISHONOR
(coming in December)

HAWK & FISHER
WOLF IN THE FOLD

SIMON R. GREEN

ACE BOOKS, NEW YORK

This book is an Ace original edition,
and has never been previously published.

WOLF IN THE FOLD

An Ace Book / published by arrangement with
the author

PRINTING HISTORY
Ace edition / September 1991

ISBN: 0-441-31835-5

Ace Books are published by The Berkley Publishing Group,
200 Madison Avenue, New York, New York 10016.
The name "ACE" and the "A" logo
are trademarks belonging to Charter Communications, Inc.

PRINTED IN THE UNITED STATES OF AMERICA

10 9 8 7 6 5 4 3 2 1

1

A Head Start

When you are tired of life, come to Haven. And someone will kill you.

The city port of Haven was a bad place to be after dark. It wasn't much better during the day. If there was a viler, more corrupt and crime-ridden city in the whole of the Low Kingdoms, its existence must have been kept secret to avoid depressing the general populace. If Haven hadn't been settled squarely on the main trade routes, and made itself such a vital part of the Low Kingdoms' economy, it would undoubtedly have been forcibly evacuated and burnt to the ground long ago, like any other plague spot. As it was, the city thrived and prospered, brimming with crime, intrigue, and general decadence.

It also made a lot of money from tourism.

Such a dangerous city needed dangerous men and women to keep it under something like control. So from Devil's Hook to the Street of Gods, from the Docks to High Tory, the city Guard patrolled the streets of Haven with cold steel always to hand, and did the best they could under impossible conditions. Apart from the murderers, muggers, rapists, and everyday scum, they were also up against organized crime, institutionalized brutality and rogue sorcerers; not to mention rampant corruption within their own ranks. They did the best they could, and for the most part learned to be content with little victories.

They should have been the best of the best: men and women with iron nerves, high morals, and implacable wills. Unstoppable heroes, ready to take on any odds to overthrow injustice. But given the low pay, appalling working conditions and high mortality rate, the Guard settled for what it could get. Most were out-of-work mercenaries, marking time until the next war, but there was always a ripe mixture of thugs, idealists, and drifters, all with their own reasons for joining a losing side. Revenge was a common motive. Haven was a breeding ground for victims.

The Guard squadroom was a large, cheerless office at the rear of Guard Headquarters. It was windowless, like the rest of the building. Windows made the place too vulnerable to assault. The Headquarters made do with narrow archery slits and ever-burning oil lamps. The walls and ceilings were covered with grime from the lamps and open fireplaces, but no one gave a damn. It fitted the general mood of the place. Half the squadroom had been taken up by oaken filing cabinets, spilling over from the cramped Records Division. At any hour of the day or night, it was a safe bet you'd find somebody desperately searching for the one piece of paper that might help them crack a case. There was a lot of useful information in the files. If you could find it. They hadn't been properly organized in over seventeen years, when most of the original files were lost in a fire-bombing.

Rumour had it that if ever the files were successfully reorganized, there'd just be another fire-bombing. So no one bothered.

And three times a day, regular as the most expensive clockwork, the squadroom filled with Guard Captains waiting for the day's briefing before going out on their shift. It was now almost ten o'clock of the evening, and twenty-eight men and women were waiting impatiently for the Guard Commander to make his appearance and give them the bad news. They knew the news would be bad. It always was.

Hawk and Fisher, husband and wife and Captains in the

Guard for more than five years, stood together at the back of the room, enjoying the warmth of the fire and trying not to think about the cold streets outside. Hawk was tall, dark, and no longer handsome. The series of old scars that marred the right side of his face gave him a bitter, sinister look, heightened by the black silk patch over his right eye. He was lean and wiry rather than muscular, and building a stomach, but even standing still the man looked dangerous. Anyone who survived five years as a Captain had to be practically unkillable, but even those who didn't know his reputation tended to give him plenty of room. There was something about Hawk, something cold and unyielding, that gave even the hardest bravo cause to think twice.

He wore the standard furs and black cloak of the Guard's winter uniform with little style and less grace. Even on a good day Hawk tended to look as though he'd got dressed in the dark. In a hurry. He wore his dark hair at shoulder length, swept back from his forehead and tied at the nape with a silver clasp. He'd only just turned thirty, but already there were streaks of grey in his hair. On his right hip Hawk carried a short-handled axe instead of a sword. He was very good with an axe. He'd had lots of practice.

Isobel Fisher leant companionably against him, putting an edge on a throwing knife with a whetstone. She was tall, easily six feet in height, and her long blond hair fell to her waist in a single thick plait, weighted at the tip with a polished steel ball. She was heading into her late twenties, and handsome rather than beautiful. There was a rawboned harshness to her face that suggested strength and stubbornness, only slightly softened by her deep blue eyes and generous mouth. Sometime in the past, something had scoured all the human weaknesses out of her, and it showed. She wore a sword on her hip in a battered scabbard, and her prowess with that blade was already legendary in a city used to legends.

A steady murmur of conversation rose and fell around Hawk and Fisher as the Guard Captains brought each other up to date on the latest gossip and exchanged ritual complaints about the lousy coffee and the necessity of working the graveyard shift. As in most cities, the night brought out the worst in Haven. But the graveyard shift paid the best, and there were always those who needed the extra money. As winter approached and the trade routes shut down one by one, choked by snow and ice and bitter storms, prices in the markets rose accordingly. Which was why every winter Hawk and Fisher, and others like them, worked from ten at night to six the next morning. And complained about it a lot.

Hawk leant back against the wall, his arms folded and his chin resting on his chest. He was never at his best at the beginning of a shift, and the recent change in schedules had just made him worse. Hawk hated having his sleeping routine changed. Fisher nudged him with her elbow, and his head came up an inch. He looked quickly round the squadroom, satisfied himself the Commander wasn't there yet, and let his chin sink back onto his chest. His eye closed. Fisher sighed, and looked away. She just hoped he wouldn't start snoring again. She checked the edge on her knife, and plucked a hair from Hawk's head to test it. He didn't react.

The door flew open and Commander Dubois stalked in, clutching a thick sheaf of papers. The Guard Captains quieted down and came to some sort of attention. Fisher put away her knife and whetstone and elbowed Hawk sharply. He straightened up with a grunt, and fixed his bleary eye on Dubois as the Commander glared out over the squadroom. Dubois was short and stocky and bald as an egg. He'd been a Commander for twenty-three years and it hadn't improved his disposition one bit. He'd been a hell of a thief-taker in his day, but he'd taken one chance too many, and half a dozen thugs took it in turn to stamp on his legs till they broke. The doctors said he'd never walk again. They didn't know Dubois. These days he spent most of his time overseeing operations, fighting the Council for a higher budget, and training new recruits. After three weeks of his slave-driving and caustic wit most recruits looked forward to hitting the streets of Haven as the lesser of two evils. It was truly said among the Guard that if you could survive Dubois, you could survive anything.

"All right; pay attention!" Dubois looked sternly about him. "First the good news: The Council's approved the money for overtime payments, starting immediately. Now the bad news: You're going to earn it. Early this morning there was a riot in the Devil's Hook. Fifty-seven dead, twenty-three injured. Two of the dead were Guards. Constables Campbell and Grzeshkowiak. Funeral's on Thursday. Those wishing to attend, line up your replacements by Tuesday latest. It's your responsibility to make sure you're covered.

"More bad news. The Dock-Workers Guild is threatening to resume their strike unless the Dock owners agree to spend more money on safe working conditions. Which means we can expect more riots. I've doubled the number of Constables in and around the Docks, but keep your eyes open. Riots have a way of spreading. And as if we didn't have enough to worry about, last night someone broke into the main catacombs on Morrison Street and removed seventy-two bodies. Could be ghouls, black magicians, or some nut cult from the Street of Gods. Either way, it's trouble. A lot of important people were buried in the catacombs, and their families are frothing at the mouth. I want those bodies back, preferably reasonably intact. Keep your ears to the ground. If you hear anything, I want to know about it.

"Now for the general reports. Captains Gibson and Doughty: Word is there's a haunted house on Blakeney Street. Check it out. If it is haunted, don't try to be heroes. Just clear the area and send for an exorcist. Captains Briars and Lee: We've had several reports of some kind of beast prowling the streets in East Gate. Only sightings so far, no attacks, but pick up silver daggers from the Armoury before you leave, just in case. Captains Fawkes and apOwen: You still haven't found that rapist yet. We've had four victims already and that's four too many. I don't care how you do it, but nail the bastard. And if someone's been shielding him, nail them too. This has top priority until I tell you otherwise.

"Captains Hawk and Fisher: Nice to have you back with us after your little holiday with the God Squad. May I remind you that in this department we prefer to bring in our perpetrators alive, whenever possible. We all know your fondness for cold steel as an answer to most problems, but try not to be so impulsive this time out. Just for me.

"Finally, we have three new rewards." He smiled humourlessly as the Captains quickly produced notepads and pencils. Rewards were one of the few legitimate perks of the job, but Dubois was of the old school and didn't approve. Rewards smelt too much like bribes to him, and distracted his men from the cases that really needed solving. He read out the reward particulars, deliberately speaking quickly to make it harder to write down the details. It didn't bother Fisher. She was a fast writer. A low rumble at her side broke her concentration, and she elbowed Hawk viciously. He snapped awake and put on his best, interested expression.

"One last item," said Dubois. "All suppressor stones are recalled, as of now. We've been having a lot of problems with them just recently. I know they've proved very useful so far in protecting us from magical attacks, but we've had a lot of reports of stones malfunctioning or otherwise proving unreliable. There's even been two cases where the damn things exploded. One Guard lost his hand. The stone blew it right off his arm. So, *all* stones are to be returned to the Armoury, as soon as possible, for checking. No exceptions. Don't make me come looking for you."

He broke off as a Constable hurried in with a sheet of paper. He passed it to Dubois, who read it quickly and then questioned the Constable in a low voice. The Captains stirred uneasily. Finally Dubois dismissed the Constable and turned back to them.

"It appears we have a spy on the loose in Haven. Nothing unusual there, but this particular spy has got his hands on some extremely sensitive material. The Council is in a panic. They want him caught, and they want him yesterday. So get out there and lean on your informants. Someone must know something. The city Gates have all been sealed, so he's not going anywhere.

"Unfortunately, the Council hasn't given us much information to go on. We know the spy's code name: Fenris.

We also have a vague description: tall and thin with blond hair. Apart from that, you're on your own. Finding this Fenris now has top priority over all other cases until we've got him, or until the Council tells us otherwise. All right, end of briefing. Get out of here. And someone wake up Hawk."

There was general laughter as the Captains dispersed, and Fisher dragged Hawk towards the door, Hawk protesting innocently that he'd heard every word. He broke off as they left the squadroom, and Fisher headed for the Armoury.

"Isobel, where are you going?"

"The Armoury. To hand in the suppressor stone."

"Forget it," said Hawk. "I'm not giving that up. It's the only protection we've got against hostile magic."

Fisher looked at him. "You heard Dubois; the damned things are dangerous. I'm not having my hand blown off, just so you can feel a bit more secure."

"All right then, I'll carry it."

"No you won't. I don't trust you with gadgets."

"Well, one of us has to have it. Or the next rogue magician we run into is going to hand us our heads. Probably literally."

Fisher sighed, and nodded reluctantly. "All right, but we only use the thing in emergencies. Agreed?"

"Agreed."

They strode unhurriedly through the narrow Headquarters corridors and out onto the crowded street. Just a few weeks ago there'd been snow and slush everywhere, but the city's weather wizards had finally got their act together and deflected the worst of the weather away from Haven, sending it out over the ocean. This wasn't making them too popular with passing merchant ships, but no one in Haven cared what they thought.

Not that the weather wizards had done anything more than buy Haven a few extra weeks, a month at most. Once the real winter storms started there was nothing anyone could do but nail up the shutters, stoke up the fire, and pray for spring. But for the moment the sky was clear, and the chilly air was no worse than an average autumn day. Hawk turned up his nose at the bracing air and pulled his cloak tightly around him. He didn't like cloaks as a rule, they got in the way during fights, but he liked the cold even less. The weather in the Low Kingdoms was generally colder and harsher than in his homeland in the North, and it was during fall and winter that he missed the Forest Kingdom most of all. He smiled sourly as he looked out over the slumped buildings and grubby streets. He was a long way from home.

"You're thinking about the Forest again, aren't you?" said Fisher.

"Yeah."

"Don't. We can't go back."

"We might. Some day."

Fisher looked at him. "Sure," she said finally. "Some day."

They strode down the packed street, the crowd giving way before them. There were a lot of people about for the time of night, but with winter so close, everyone was desperate to get as much done as they could before the storms descended and the streets became impassable. Hawk and Fisher smiled and nodded to familiar faces, and slowly made their way into the Northside, their beat and one of the worst areas in Haven. You could buy or sell anything there; every dirty little trade, every shape and form of evil and corruption grew and flourished in the dark and grimy streets of the Northside. Hawk and Fisher, who had worked the area for over five years, had grown blasé and hardened despite themselves. Yet every day the Northside came up with new things to shock them. They tried hard not to let it get to them.

They made a tour of all the usual dives, looking for word on the spy Fenris, but to a man everyone they talked to swore blind they'd never even heard of the fellow. Hawk and Fisher took turns smashing up furniture and glaring up close at those they questioned, but not even their reputations could scare up any information. Which meant that either the spy had gone to ground so thoroughly that no one knew where he was, or his masters were paying out a small fortune in bribes to keep people's mouths shut. Probably the former. There was always someone in the Northside who'd talk.

They left the Inn of the Black Freighter till last. It was a semirespectable tavern and restaurant right on the outer edge of the Northside; the kind of place where you paid through the nose for out-of-season delicacies, and the waiter sneered at you if your accent slipped. It was also a clearing house for information, gossip, and rumour, all for sale on a sliding scale that started at expensive and rose quickly to extortionate. Hawk and Fisher looked in from time to time to pick up the latest information, and never paid a penny. Instead, they let their informants live and promised not to set fire to the building on the way out.

They stood outside the Black Freighter a moment, listening to the sounds of conversation and laughter carry softly on the night air. It seemed there was a good crowd in tonight. They pushed open the door and strolled in, smiling graciously about them. The headwaiter started towards them, his hand positioned just right for a surreptitious bribe for a good table, and then he stopped dead, his face falling as he saw who it was. A sudden silence fell across the tavern, and a sea of sullen faces glared at Hawk and Fisher from the dimly lit tables. As in most restaurants, the lighting was kept to a minimum. Officially, this was to provide an intimate, romantic atmosphere. Hawk thought it was because if the customers could see what they were eating, they wouldn't pay for it. But then he was no romantic, as Fisher would be the first to agree.

The quiet was complete, save for the crackling of the fire at the end of the room, and the atmosphere was so tense you could have struck a match off it. Hawk and Fisher headed for the bar, which boasted richly polished chrome and veneer and all the latest fashionable spirits and liqueurs, lined up in neat, orderly rows. A large mirror covered most of the wall behind the bar, surrounded by rococo scrollwork of gold and silver.

Hawk and Fisher leaned on the bar and smiled companionably at the bartender, Howard, who looked as though he would have very much liked to turn and run, but didn't dare. He swallowed once, gave the bartop a quick polish it didn't need, and smiled fixedly at the two Guards. He might have been handsome in his heyday, but twenty years of more than good living had buried those good looks under too much weight, and his smile was weak now, from having been too many things to too many people. He had a wife and a mistress who fought loudly in public, and many other signs of success, but though he now owned the Inn where he'd once been nothing more than a lowly waiter, he still liked to spend most of his time behind the bar, keeping an eye on things. None of his staff was going to sneak up on him, the way he had on the previous owner. Hawk shifted his weight slightly, and the bartender jumped in spite of himself. Hawk smiled.

"Good crowd in tonight, Howard. How's business?"

"Fine! Just fine," said Howard quickly. "Couldn't be better. Can I get you a drink? Or a table? Or . . . Oh hell, Hawk, you're not going to bust up the place again, are you? I only just finished redecorating from the last time you were here, and those mirrors are expensive. And you know the insurance people won't pay out if you're involved. They class you and Fisher along with storm damage, rogue magic, and Acts of Gods."

"No need to be so worried, Howard," said Fisher. "Anyone would think you had something to hide."

"Look, I just run the place. No one tells me anything. You know that."

"We're looking for someone," said Hawk. "Fenris. It's a spy's code name. You ever heard it before?"

"No," said the bartender quickly. "Never. If I had, I'd tell you, word of honour. I don't have any truck with spies. I'm a patriotic man, always have been, loyal as the day is long. . . ."

"Pack it in," said Fisher. "We believe you, though thousands wouldn't. Who's in tonight that might know something?"

Howard hesitated, and Hawk frowned at him. The bartender swallowed hard. "There's Fast Tommy, the Little Lord, and Razor Eddie. It's just possible they might have heard a thing or two. . . ."

Hawk nodded, and turned away from the bar to stare out

over the restaurant. People had started eating again, but the place was still silent as the tomb, save for the odd clatter of cutlery on plates. It didn't take him long to spot the three faces Howard had named. They were all quite well known, in their way. Hawk and Fisher had met them before; in their line of business, it was inevitable.

"Thank you, Howard," said Hawk. "You've been a great help. Now, tell that bouncer of yours, who thinks he's hidden behind the pillar to our left, that if he doesn't put down that throwing knife and step into plain sight, Isobel and I are going to cut him off at the knees."

Howard made a quick gesture, and the bouncer stepped reluctantly into view, his hands conspicuously empty. "Sorry," said the bartender. "He's new."

"He'd better learn fast," said Fisher. "Or he's never going to be old."

They turned their backs on Howard and the bouncer, and threaded their way through the packed tables. Glaring faces and hostile eyes followed the two Captains as they headed for Fast Tommy's table. As usual, Tommy was dressed in the height of last month's fashion, had enough heavy rings on his fingers to double as knuckle-dusters, and was accompanied by a gorgeous young blonde half falling out of her dress. Tommy glared at Hawk and Fisher as they pulled up chairs opposite him, but made no objections. He undoubtedly had a bodyguard or two somewhere nearby but had enough sense not to call them. Hawk and Fisher might have taken that as an affront, and then he'd have had to find some new bodyguards. No one messed with Hawk and Fisher. It was quicker and a lot safer just to tell them what they wanted to know, and hope they'd go away and bother someone else.

Fast Tommy was a gambling man. He got his name as a lightning calculator, though some uncharitable souls suggested it had more to do with his love life. He was a short, squarish, dark-haired man in his early forties, with a gambler's easy smile and unreadable eyes. He nodded politely to Hawk and Fisher.

"My dear Captains, so good to see you again. May I

purchase you wine, or cigars? Perhaps a little hot chocolate; very warming in the inclement weather . . ."

"Tell us about the spy, Tommy," said Hawk.

"I'm afraid the name Fenris is unknown to me, Captain, but I can of course inquire of my associates. . . ."

"You're holding out on us, Tommy," said Fisher reproachfully. "You know how it upsets us when you do that."

"Upon my sweet mother's grave . . ."

"Your mother is alive and well and still paying interest on the last loan you made her," said Hawk.

Fisher looked thoughtfully at the gambler's blond companion. "Little old for you, isn't she, Tommy? She must be all of seventeen. Maybe we should check our records, make sure she isn't some underage runaway."

The young blonde smiled sweetly at Fisher, and lifted her wineglass so she could show off the heavy gold bracelet at her wrist.

"She's sixteen," said Tommy quickly. "I've seen the birth certificate." He swallowed hard, and smiled determinedly at the two Guards. "Believe me, my dear friends, I know nothing of this Fenris person. . . ."

"But you can find out," said Hawk. "Leave word at Guard Headquarters, when you know something."

"Of course, Captain, of course . . ."

Fisher leaned forward. "If we find out later that you've been holding something back from us . . ."

"Do I look suicidal?" said Fast Tommy.

Hawk and Fisher got to their feet, and made their way through the tangle of tables to join the Little Lord in her private booth at the back. No one knew the Little Lord's real name, but then, nobody cared that much. Aliases were as common as fleas in the Northside, and a damn sight easier to live with. The Lord was a tall, handsome woman in her mid-thirties who always dressed as a man. She had close-cropped dark hair, a thin slash of a mouth, and dark piercing eyes. She dressed smartly but formally, in that old male style that never really goes out of fashion, and affected an upper class accent that was only occasionally successful.

She always had money, though no one knew where it came from. Truth be told, most people weren't sure they wanted to know. She peered short-sightedly at Hawk and Fisher as they sat down opposite her, and screwed a monocle into her left eye.

"As I live and breathe, Captain Hawk and Captain Fisher. Damned fine to see you again. Care to join me in a glass of bubbly?"

Hawk eyed the half bottle of pink champagne in the nearby ice bucket, and shuddered briefly. "Not right now, thank you. What can you tell us about the spy Fenris?"

"Not a damned thing, old boy. Don't really move in those circles, you know."

"You're looking very smart," said Fisher. "Those diamond cuff links are new, aren't they?"

"Present from me dear auntie. The old girl and I were up at Lord Bruford's the other day, meeting that new Councillor chappie. Adamant, I think his name was...."

"Never mind the social calendar," said Fisher. "A set of matched diamonds disappeared mysteriously during a Society bash last week. You wouldn't know anything about that, I suppose?"

"Not a thing, m'dear. Shocked to hear it, of course."

"Of course," said Hawk. "Are you sure you haven't heard something about Fenris, my Lord? After all, someone such as yourself, moving in your circles, would be bound to hear something; perhaps spoken in confidence in an unguarded moment?"

The Little Lord raised an elegant eyebrow, and her monocle fell out. She caught it deftly before it hit the tabletop, and screwed it back in place. "My dear chap, surely you're not asking me to peach on a friend? Just ain't done, you know."

"Those diamond cuff links are looking more and more familiar," said Fisher. "Perhaps the three of us should take a little walk down to Headquarters, so we can compare them with the artist's rendering of the missing items...."

"I assure you, Captain, I haven't heard a thing about your beastly spy! But of course I'd be only too happy to keep my eyes and ears alert for any morsel of gossip that might float my way.''

"That's the spirit," said Hawk. "Noblesse oblige, right? And by the way, I've met Councillor Adamant, and I know for a fact he's never bloody heard of you.''

He and Fisher left the spluttering Lord in her booth, and made their way through the last of the tables to their final port of call, a single table at the rear of the tavern, half hidden in shadows. Razor Eddie wasn't fond of even dim light. Hawk and Fisher borrowed chairs from nearby tables, and sat down facing him. Razor Eddie was a slight, hunched figure wrapped in a tattered grey cloak apparently held together only by accumulated filth and grease. Even across a table the smell was appalling. He was said to be so dirty, plague rats wouldn't go near him in case they caught something. He was painfully thin, with a hollowed face and fever-bright eyes. At first glance he looked like just another down and out, but you only had to be in the man's presence a few moments to know there was something special about him. Special . . . and not a little disturbing.

Razor Eddie got his name in a street fight over territory between two neighbouring gangs. He was fourteen at the time, a slick and vicious killer, and already more than a little crazy. He spent the next few years working for anyone who'd have him, just for the action. And then, at the age of seventeen, he visited the Street of Gods and got religion in a big way. He turned his back on his violent past and walked the streets of the Northside, preaching love and understanding. A few people laughed at him, and threw things. Later, they were found dead, under mysterious circumstances. They weren't the last. After a while people learned to leave Razor Eddie strictly alone. He walked through the most dangerous areas in Haven, spreading his message, and came out unscathed. Once, a gang of ten bravos went into the Devil's Hook after him. No one ever saw them again. Razor Eddie had no fixed abode or territory; he slept in doorways and wandered where he would. Neither heat nor cold affected him, and he always seemed to have a little money, even in the hardest of times.

He knew a lot of things, about a lot of people—if you could persuade him to talk. Most couldn't, but he'd taken a shine to Hawk and Fisher. Probably because unlike most other people, they weren't frightened of him. Hawk leant back in his chair and smiled easily at the hunched figure opposite him.

"Hello, Eddie. How's life treating you?"

"Mustn't grumble, Captain," said Razor Eddie. His voice was low and calm and very reasonable, but his eyes shone with a wild light. "There's always someone worse off than yourself. I've been waiting for you. You'll find the spy Fenris in the house with three gables on Leech Street. He uses it as a drop for passing information. You'll know Fenris by his bright green cravat. It's a signal for his contact."

"You're not normally this forthcoming, Eddie," said Fisher, frowning. "What's so special about this Fenris?"

"Unless someone stops him, two great houses will go down in flames. Blood will run in gutters and the screams will never end. There are wolves running loose among the flock, and they will bring us all down."

Hawk and Fisher looked at each other briefly, and when they looked back, Razor Eddie's chair was empty. They looked quickly about them, but there was no sign of him anywhere in the tavern.

"I hate it when he does that," said Fisher. "Well, what do you think? Is it worth a trip to Leech Street?"

Hawk scowled. "Anyone else, I'd take it with a pinch of salt. But Eddie's different. He knows things. And if he thinks we're all in danger because of this Fenris . . ."

"Yeah," said Fisher. "Worrying, that."

"It's the best lead we've got."

"It's the only lead we've got."

"Exactly."

Fisher shook her head. "Let's go check it out."

They grinned at each other, got up, and made their way back through the crowded tables. The restaurant was still utterly silent, their every move followed by hostile eyes. They got to the door, and Hawk paused and looked back.

He smiled, and bowed courteously to the sea of unfriendly faces. Fisher blew the room a kiss, and then the two Guards disappeared into the night.

Leech Street was bold and brassy and more than a little shop-soiled. Brightly painted whores gathered together on street corners like so many raucous birds of paradise, or leaned out of first-floor windows in revealing underwear, watching the world go by with knowing mascarad eyes. Street traders hawked jewelry so freshly stolen the true owners hadn't even realized it was gone yet, and hole-in-the-wall taverns provided cheap shots of spirits so rough they all but seethed in the bottle. The air was full of chatter and laughter and the harsh banter of the strip-show barkers. Here and there, gaudily dressed pimps leant casually in open doorways, ostentatiously cleaning their fingernails with the point of a knife, alert for the first sign of trouble. Prospective clients, trying to appear anonymous, thronged one end of the street to the other, eyeing the various merchandise and working up their courage to the sticking point.

Hawk, watching the bustling scene from the concealing shadows of an alley mouth, yawned widely. He and Fisher had been in position for almost an hour waiting for Fenris to show up, and what little tawdry glamour the street possessed had long since worn thin. When you got past the noise and the bright colors, Leech Street seemed more sad and sleazy than anything else, with everyone trying desperately to pretend they were something other than what they really were. Hawk derived some amusement from the attempts of most of the would-be customers to give the impression they just happened to be passing through, but the street itself held no attractions for him. He'd seen the official figures on violence and robbery in this area, not to mention venereal disease. In some establishments, the crabs were reputed to be so big they jumped out on dithering passersby and dragged them bodily inside.

Bored, Hawk leant gingerly back against the grimy alley wall and kicked at an empty bottle on the ground. It rolled slowly away, hesitated, and then rolled back again. After a fruitless hour standing watch, this was almost exciting. Hawk sighed deeply. He hated doing stakeouts. He didn't have the patience for it. Fisher, on the other hand, actually seemed to enjoy it these days. She'd taken to watching the passersby and making up little histories about who they were and where they were going. Her stories were invariably more interesting than the case they were working on, but now, after a solid hour of listening to them, Hawk found their charm wearing a bit thin. Fisher chattered on, blithely unknowing, while Hawk's scowl deepened. His stomach rumbled loudly, reminding him of missed meals. Fisher broke off suddenly, and Hawk quickly looked round, worried she'd noticed his inattention, but her gaze was fixed on something down the street.

"I think we've finally struck gold, Hawk. Green cravat at three o'clock."

Hawk followed her gaze, and his interest stirred. "Think he's our man?"

"Would you wear a cravat like that if you didn't have to?"

Hawk smiled. She had a point. The cravat was so bright and virulent a green it practically glowed. The suspect looked casually about him, ignoring the birdlike calls of the whores. He fit the description, what there was of it. He was definitely tall, easily six foot three or four, and decidedly lean. His clothes, apart from the cravat, were tastefully bland, with nothing about them to identify the kind of man who wore them. For a moment his gaze fell upon the alley from which Hawk was watching. Hawk damped down an impulse to shrink further back into the shadows; the movement would only draw attention to him. The spy's gaze moved on, and Hawk breathed a little more easily.

"All right," said Fisher. "Let's get him."

"Hold your horses," said Hawk. "We want whoever he's here to meet as well, not just him. Let's give him a minute, and see what happens."

One of the bolder whores advanced aggressively towards the spy. He smiled at her and said something that made her laugh, and she turned away. *He can't just stand around much longer,* thought Hawk. *That would be bound to attract attention. So what the hell's he waiting for?* Even as the thought crossed Hawk's mind, the spy turned suddenly and walked over to a building on the opposite side of the street. He produced a key, unlocked the door and slipped quickly inside, pulling the door shut behind him. Hawk counted ten slowly to himself and then stepped out of the alley, Fisher at his side. The house the spy had gone into looked just like all the others on the street.

"I'll take the front," said Hawk. "You cover the back, in case he tries to make a run for it."

"How come I always have to cover the back?" said Fisher. "I always end up in someone's back yard, trying to fight my way through three weeks' accumulated garbage."

"All right. You take the front and I'll cover the back."

"Oh no; it's too late now. You should have thought of it without me having to tell you."

Hawk gave her an exasperated look, but she was already heading for the narrow alley at the side of the building. Sometimes you just couldn't talk to Fisher. Hawk turned his attention back to the house's front door as it loomed up before him. A faded sign hanging above the door gave the name of the place as MISTRESS LUCY'S ESTABLISHMENT. The sign boasted a portrait of the lady herself, which suggested she'd looked pretty faded even when the sign was new. Hawk casually tried the handle. It turned easily in his grasp, but the door wouldn't open. Locked. Surprise, surprise. Maybe he should have let Fisher have the front door after all. She was a lot better at picking locks than he.

On the other hand . . . When in doubt, be direct.

He knocked politely on the door, and waited. There was a pause and then the door swung open, and a hand shot out and fastened on his arm. Hawk jumped in spite of himself, and his hand started towards his axe before he realized the person before him was very definitely not the spy Fenris. Instead, Hawk found himself facing a large, heavy-set woman wrapped in gaudy robes, with a wild frizz of dark curly hair and so much makeup it was almost impossible to make out her features. Her smile was a wide scarlet gash and her eyes were bright and piercing. Her shoulders were as wide as a docker's, and she had arms to match. The hand on his arm closed fiercely, and he winced.

"I'm glad you're here," said the woman earnestly. "We've been waiting for you."

Hawk looked at her blankly. "You have?"

"Of course. But we must hurry. The spirits are restless tonight."

Hawk wondered if things might become a little clearer if he went away and came back again later. Like maybe next year.

"Spirits," he said, carefully.

The woman looked at him sharply. "You are here for the sitting, aren't you?"

"I don't think so," said Hawk.

The woman let go of his arm as though he'd just made an indecent proposal, drew herself up to her full five-foot-nine, and fixed him with a steely glare. "Do I understand that you are not Jonathan DeQuincey, husband of the late and much lamented Dorothy DeQuincey?"

"Yes," said Hawk. That much he was sure of.

"Then if you have not come to see me in my capacity as Madam Zara, Spirit Guide and Pathway to the Great Beyond, why are you here?"

"You mean you're a spiritualist?" said Hawk, the light slowly dawning. "A medium?"

"Not just *a* medium, young man; the foremost practitioner of the Art in all Haven."

"Then why are you based here, instead of on the Street of Gods?" asked Hawk innocently.

Madam Zara sniffed haughtily. "Certain closed minds on the Council refuse to accept spiritualists as genuine wonderworkers. They dare to accuse us of being fakes and frauds. We, of course, know different. It's all part of a conspiracy by the established religions to prevent us taking our rightful place on the Street of Gods. Now, what do you want? I can't stand around here chatting with you; the Great Beyond calls . . . and I have customers waiting."

"I'm looking for the gentleman who just came in here," said Hawk. "Tall, thin, wears a green cravat. I have a message for him."

"Oh, him." Madam Zara turned up her nose regally. "Upstairs, second on the left. And you can tell the young 'gentleman' his rent's due."

She turned her back on Hawk in a swirl of billowing robes, and marched off down the narrow hall. Hawk stepped inside and shut the door quietly behind him. By the time he turned back, Madam Zara had disappeared, presumably to rejoin her clients, and the hall was empty. A single lamp shed a dirty yellow glow over a row of coats and cloaks on the left-hand wall and a tattily carpeted stairway that lead up to the next floor. Hawk took a small wooden wedge from his pocket and jammed it firmly under the front door. That should slow Fenris down if he made a run for it. Hawk carried lots of useful things in his pockets. He believed in being prepared.

He drew his axe. The odds were that the spy Fenris was alone with his contact. He wouldn't want to risk unnecessary witnesses. So, two-to-one odds. Hawk grinned, and hefted his axe. No problem. Things were looking up. If he and Fisher could bring in both the spy and his contact alive and ready for questioning, then maybe he and Fisher could finally get transferred out of the Northside permanently. . . .

He padded silently forward, and made his way slowly up the stairs. With any luck, even if the spy had heard him at the door, he'd just assume Hawk was another of Madam Zara's clients. Which should give Hawk the advantage of surprise if it came to a fight. Hawk firmly believed in making use of every possible advantage when it came to a fight. He ascended the stairs slowly, checking each step first to see if it was likely to creak. He had a lot of experience when it came to sneaking around houses, and he knew how far a sudden sound could carry on the quiet.

He reached the landing without incident and padded silently over to the second door on the left. Light shone around the doorframe. He put his ear to the wood, and smiled as he heard a voice raised loudly in argument. He stepped back, hefted his axe once, and braced himself to kick in the door. At which point the door swung open, revealing the spy Fenris standing in the doorway with a startled expression. For a moment he and Hawk just stood there, staring at each other, and then Hawk launched himself at the spy. Fenris fell back, shock and alarm fighting for control of his features. Hawk glanced quickly round the room, and his gaze fell on the spy's contact—a grey, anonymous man with an icily calm face.

"Stand where you are, both of you!" barked Hawk. "You're under arrest. Throw down your weapons!"

The contact drew his sword and advanced on Hawk. The spy fumbled for a throwing knife. *Oh hell,* thought Hawk tiredly, *Just once, why can't they do the sensible thing and give up without a fight?* He decided he'd better take out the contact first; he looked to be the more dangerous of the two. Once the contact had been subdued, Fenris would likely give himself up without a struggle. Hawk closed in on the contact; the man's face was utterly bland and forgettable, but his eyes were cold and deadly calm. Hawk began to have a very bad feeling about him. He pushed the thought aside and launched his attack. The grey man brushed aside Hawk's axe effortlessly, and Hawk had to retreat rapidly to avoid being transfixed by the contact's follow-through.

The grey man moved quickly after him, cutting and thrusting with awesome skill, and it was all Hawk could do to hold him off. Fenris' contact was an expert swordsman. Hawk's heart sank. When all was said and done, an axe was not designed as a defensive weapon. Hawk usually won his fights by launching an all-out attack and not letting up until his opponent was beaten. As it was, only frantic footwork and some inspired use of the axe was keeping him alive. Hawk had been an excellent swordsman in his younger days, before he lost his eye, but even then he would have been hard pressed to beat the grey man. He was fast, brilliant, and disturbingly methodical. Unless Hawk could come up with something in a hurry, he was a dead man, and both he and the grey man knew it. Out of the corner of his eye, Hawk could see Fenris circling around them with a throwing knife in his hand, looking for an opening. That settled it. When in doubt, fight dirty.

He struck at the grey man's head with his axe, forcing him to raise his sword to parry the blow, and while the two blades were engaged, Hawk pivoted neatly on one foot and kicked the grey man squarely in the groin. The man's face paled and his sword arm wavered. Hawk brought his axe across in a sudden, savage blow that sliced through the man's throat. Blood spurted thickly as the grey man collapsed. Hawk spun quickly to face Fenris. He might have lost the contact, but he was damned if he'd lose the spy as well. Fenris aimed and threw his knife in a single fluid movement. Hawk threw himself to one side, and the knife shot past his shoulder but pinned his cloak firmly to the wall. Hawk scrabbled frantically at the cloak's clasp as Fenris turned and bolted out the door. Some days, nothing goes right.

The clasp finally came undone, and he jerked free, leaving the cloak hanging pinned to the wall behind him. He charged out of the room and onto the landing. He'd come back for the cloak later. He peered over the banister and caught a glimpse of Fenris standing at the foot of the stairs, looking frantically about him. Hawk clattered down the stairs, cursing quietly to himself. He hated chases. He was built for stamina, not speed, and he was already out of breath from the exertions of the fight. Still, Fenris wouldn't get that far. The wedge under the front door should see to that.

In the darkened parlour, the seance was well under way. A mysterious pool of light illuminated a small circular table, throwing sinister shadows on the faces of the six people gathered hopefully around it. Darkness pressed close about the circle of light, hiding the pokey little parlour and giving the six participants a feeling of being adrift in eternity. The air was heavy with the scent of sandalwood, and over all there was an atmosphere of unease and anticipation. Madam Zara rocked back and forth on her chair, as though all around her spirits were jostling for possession of her voice, desperate to pass on messages of hope and comfort to those they had left behind. Madam Zara's head lolled limply on her neck, but her eyes kept a careful if unobtrusive watch on her clients.

It was just her regulars this week. The Holbrooks, a middle-aged couple wanting to contact their dead son. David and Mercy Peyton, still hopeful their dear departed grandfather would reveal to them where he'd hidden the family fortune. And old Mrs. Tyrell, timidly grateful for any fleeting contact with her dead cat, Marmalade. The two couples were easy enough; all they needed were general platitudes on the one hand and vague hints on the other, but having to make cat noises was downright demeaning. If trade hadn't dropped off so much recently she'd have drawn the line at pets, but times were hard, and Madam Zara had to make do with what she could get.

She let her eyes roll back in her head, and produced her best sepulchral moan. She was rather proud of her moan. It had something of the mystic and the eternal in it, and was guaranteed to make even the most skeptical client sit up and take notice. She took a firm grip on the hands of Graeme Holbrook and David Peyton on either side of her, and let a delicate shudder run down her arms into her hands.

"The spirits are with us," she said softly. "They are near us in everything we do, separated from us by only the thinnest of veils. They wish always to make contact with us, and all we have to do is listen. . . . Hush. I feel a disturbance in the ether. A spirit draws near. Speak with my voice, dear departed one. Have you a message for someone here?"

The atmosphere grew taut and strained as Madam Zara threw in a few more moans and shivers, and then pressed her foot firmly onto the lever hidden in the floorboards. A block of wood thudded hollowly against the underside of the table, making the clients jump. She hit the lever a few more times, producing more mysterious knockings, and then concentrated on getting the right intonations for the Peyton grandfather's voice. People didn't appreciate what mediums had to go through for their money. She could have been a legitimate actress, if only she'd had the breaks.

"The spirit is drawing closer. I can feel a presence in the room. It's almost here. . . ."

The door flew open and the tall thin gentleman from upstairs charged in, glared wildly about him, and then headed for the window. The Holbrooks screamed, and Mercy Peyton fell backwards off her chair. Madam Zara looked confusedly about her, completely thrown. Another figure burst in through the open door, his clothes soaked with blood, fresh gore dripping from the axe in his hand. The Holbrooks screamed even louder and clutched each other tightly, convinced that the Grim Reaper himself had come to claim them for meddling in his affairs. The gentleman from upstairs threw open the window and slung a leg over the windowsill. The second figure charged forward, overturning the table. He grabbed at the young gentleman's shoulder, and just missed as he dropped into the alleyway outside. The second figure cursed horribly and clambered out the window in hot pursuit. The Holbrooks were still clutching each other and whimpering, Mercy Peyton was having hysterics, loudly, and David Peyton was thoughtfully examining the block of wood on the underside of the overturned table. Madam Zara searched frantically for something to say that would retrieve the situation. And just at that moment a large orange cat jumped in through the window from the alley outside and looked around to see what all the fuss was about. Mrs. Tyrell snatched him up and hugged him to her with tears of joy in her eyes.

"Marmalade! You've come back to me!"

Madam Zara mentally washed her hands of the whole situation.

Out in the alley, Hawk found Fisher picking herself up out of a pile of garbage. He started forward to help, and then hesitated as the smell hit him. Fisher glared at him.

"Next time, you're going to watch the back door."

She headed quickly for the main street, brushing herself off as she went. Hawk hurried after her.

"Did you see Fenris?"

"Of course I saw him! Who do you think knocked me

into the garbage? And whatever you're about to say, I don't
want to hear it. How was I to know he'd come flying out
of a window? Now, let's move it. He can't be more than a
few minutes ahead of us.''

They pounded down the alley and out into Leech Street.
Fenris was halfway down the street and running well. Hawk
and Fisher charged after him. The crowds turned to watch.
Some laughed, a few cheered, and the rest yelled insults
and placed bets. A few up ahead took in Fisher's black
cloak and moved to block the street. Guards weren't much
respected in Leech Street. Hawk glared at them.

''We're Hawk and Fisher, city Guard. Get the hell out
of the way!''

The crowd parted suddenly before them, falling back on
all sides to give them plenty of room. Fenris glanced back
over his shoulder and redoubled his efforts. Fisher nodded
approvingly at the more respectful crowd.

''I think they've heard of us, Hawk.''

''Shut up and keep running.''

Fenris darted down a side alley, and Hawk and Fisher
plunged in after him. Hawk was already breathing hard.
Fenris led them through a twisting maze of narrow streets
and back alleys, changing direction and doubling back
whenever he could. Hawk and Fisher stuck doggedly with
him, breath burning in their lungs and sweat running down
their heaving sides. Fenris ran through a street market, overturning stalls as he went, to try and slow them down. Hawk
just ploughed right through the wreckage, with Fisher close
behind. Furious stallholders shook their fists and called
down curses on the heads of pursued and pursuers alike.

Hawk's scowl deepened as he ran. Fenris was leading
them deep into the rotten heart of the Northside, but Hawk
was damned if he could figure out exactly where the man
was headed. He must have some destination in mind, some
bolt-hole he could hide in, or a friend who'd protect him.
Hawk smiled nastily. He didn't care if the spy ended up in
the Hall of Justice, protected by all twelve Judges and the
King himself; Fenris was going to gaol, preferably in chains.

It had become a matter of honour. Not to mention revenge. Hawk hated chases.

And then Fenris rounded a corner at full speed, and darted up an exterior stairway on a large squat building of stained and patterned stone. Hawk started after him, but Fisher grabbed him by the arm and brought them both to a sudden halt. Fenris disappeared through a door into the building. Hawk turned on Fisher.

"Before you say anything, Hawk. Look where we are."

Hawk glared around him, and then grimaced, his anger draining quickly away. Fenris had brought them to Magus Court, home to all the lowlife magicians and sorcerers in Haven. The place looked deserted for the moment, but that could change in a second. On the whole, Guards tended to walk very quietly in and around Magus Court and not draw attention to themselves. Certainly, no one ever tried to make arrests there without massive support from the Guard, and, if necessary, the army. Otherwise they'd have been safer playing brass instruments in a cave full of hibernating bears.

"That's not all," said Fisher. "Look whose house he's holed up in."

Hawk looked, and groaned. "Grimm," he said disgustedly. "All the magic-users Fenris could have known, and it had to be the sorcerer Grimm."

He and Fisher leant against the wall at the bottom of the exterior stairway and grabbed a few minutes' rest while they tried to work out what the hell to do next. Hawk and Fisher knew Grimm, and he knew them. They'd crossed swords before, metaphorically speaking, but Hawk and Fisher had never been able to pin anything on him. People were too scared to talk.

Grimm was a medium-level sorcerer with unpleasant personal habits who specialized in shape changing. He could do anything from a face-lift to a full body transformation, depending on the needs, and wealth, of his client. He had no scruples; he'd do anything, to anyone. Criminals found his services very useful, either for themselves, to change an appearance that had grown too well-known, or for taking revenge on their enemies. The Guard had found one up-

and-coming crime boss wandering the streets in the early hours of the morning, leaving a bloody trail behind him. It took them some time to identify him. He'd been flayed, every inch of skin removed from head to toe, but he was still alive, and screaming. He took a long time to die in the main city hospital, and he only stopped screaming when his voice gave out.

It figured Fenris would know someone like Grimm. All the spy had to do was acquire a new face and build and he could disappear into the crowds right under Hawk's and Fisher's noses. On the other hand, they couldn't just go barging in after him. Grimm was a sorcerer and took his privacy very seriously. Officially, any Guard could enter any premises in Haven, providing they could demonstrate good cause in the Courts afterwards. In practice, it all depended on whose home you were talking about. Having a Court declare you posthumously correct wasn't much of a comfort, and sorcerers tended to throw spells first and think afterwards. Constant industrial espionage among magic-users had produced a general paranoia and split-second reflexes.

"What do you think?" said Hawk finally.

"I think we should think about this very carefully," said Fisher. "I have no desire to spend the rest of my life as a combination of several small, unpleasant, and very smelly animals. Shapechange sorcerers are renowned for having a very warped sense of humour. I say we stay put and call for backup."

"By the time anyone gets here, Fenris will have his new face and we'll have lost him."

Fisher scowled. "Given the alternatives, I say let him go. It's not as if he was a murderer or something. Hell, Haven's full of spies. What's one more or less going to make any difference?"

"No," said Hawk firmly. "We can't let him go. It would be bad for our reputation. People would think we'd got soft, and take advantage."

Fisher shook her head. "There has to be an easier way to make a living. All right, let's go in after him. No point in sneaking around. Grimm's bound to have the place covered with security spells to warn of intruders. So, crash straight in and trust to the suppressor stone to protect us. Right?''

"Sounds good to me," said Hawk. "Let's do it."

He handed Fisher the suppressor stone, and she muttered the activating phrase. The stone glowed fiercely in her hand like a miniature star. They started up the exterior stairway, Hawk in the lead, axe at the ready. The stairs creaked loudly. *Great,* thought Hawk, *Just great.* They hurried up the steps to the door at the top of the stairway. Hawk listened carefully, his ear pressed against the wood, but he couldn't hear anything. He tried the door handle and it turned stiffly in his grasp. He eased the door open an inch, and then stepped back. He glanced at Fisher for reassurance, and found she was doing the same to him. He smiled briefly. They both counted to three under their breath, kicked the door in and burst into the room beyond, weapons at the ready.

The sorcerer Grimm was escorting a robed and hooded figure to a door at the far end of the room. He spun round and glared at the intruders, and then pushed the hooded figure towards the far door. The Guards started forward, but the figure was out the door and gone before they got anywhere near him. Which left them facing the sorcerer. Grimm was a huge, broad-chested man dressed in sorcerer's black, with a thick beard and an impressive mane of jet-black hair. He was smiling unpleasantly, like a vulture about to feed on a dead man's eyes.

"You're under arrest, in the name of the Guard!" said Hawk resolutely, and then flung himself to one side as Grimm snatched a ball of fire out of thin air and threw it at him. The fireball hit a chair and incinerated it. Fisher threw a knife while the sorcerer was distracted, and it sank deep into Grimm's arm. He cursed briefly, pulled the knife out, and threw it aside. Hawk and Fisher charged across the room towards him. The sorcerer drew himself up and spoke a Word of Power. The suppressor stone flared up, cancelling out his magic. Hawk and Fisher hit the sorcerer together, throwing him to the floor. There was a short, confused struggle, and then Fisher clubbed him unconscious with the hilt of her sword. Grimm went limp, and Hawk and Fisher rolled off him. They sat together, backs against the wall, and waited for their breathing to get back to normal.

"Well, at least we've got something to show for the chase," said Hawk.

"Yeah," said Fisher. "Pity about Fenris, though. We were that close to getting him. . . ."

"Forget it," said Hawk. "He's long gone by now, with a new face and build, the crafty bastard. We'll have to start over from scratch."

"Right. Our superiors are not going to be pleased with us."

They sat in silence for a while.

"There isn't a reward on Grimm, by any chance, is there?" said Hawk hopefully.

"No chance. There's never been any real evidence against him. Still, he's dropped himself right in it this time. Aiding and abetting a fugitive, resisting arrest, assaulting the Guard . . ."

"Right," said Hawk. "Once he wakes up, he's going to have some very leading questions to answer."

"Assuming he hasn't got concussion, and lost his memory."

Hawk groaned. "Don't. It would be just our luck if we had accidentally scrambled his brains. Come on, let's have a look round the place while we're here. Maybe we'll get lucky and find a clue or something."

They moved cautiously round Grimm's quarters, being very careful not to touch anything without checking it out first. Magic-users were often fond of setting booby traps for the unwary. Hawk's usual method of searching the premises was to trash the place until it looked like a hurricane had hit it, but this room already looked as if someone had beaten him to it. Grimm was one of those people who lived in a permanent mess and liked it that way. His quarters took up the whole of the first floor—a single long room littered with junk and debris of every description.

There were racks of chemicals, glass vials and tubing, pewter mugs and mixing bowls, all scattered over two huge tables. Together with papers and books and what appeared to be the remains of at least three different meals. Hawk tossed aside a discarded shirt and grimaced as he discovered a dead cat, dissected into its component parts and neatly pinned to a display board. Beneath the cat were detailed instructions on how to put the animal back together again. Either Grimm had a really nasty sense of humour, or . . . Hawk decided very firmly that he wasn't going to think about that.

The bed looked as though Grimm had left it exactly as he'd crawled out of it. Fisher peered underneath, just in case, but there was nothing there except dust and a chamber pot. A combination desk and writing table looked more interesting. She eased the drawers open one by one with the tip of her sword, and smiled as she came across a thick sheaf of papers. She ran the suppressor stone over the desk, and then carefully removed the papers, watching all the time in case there was a mechanical booby trap as well. She leafed quickly through the papers, scowling as she tried to make out Grimm's scratchy handwriting.

Hawk looked into a recessed alcove, and his breath caught in his throat. A dozen different faces lined the wall; skins so skillfully taken and mounted they seemed almost alive. Hawk fought down his disgust and looked them over carefully. They were all unique, no two even remotely alike. Presumably they were models for the faces Grimm could give his customers. He'd better get a Guard sketch artist in to make copies. Fenris might be wearing one of these faces. He moved closer and studied them thoughtfully. Whatever else you could say about Grimm, he knew his stuff. The faces were incredibly lifelike. He reached out a hand to touch one, and then snatched his hand back as the face opened its eyes and looked at him. A grimace of pain moved slowly across the flat features, and the mouth stretched in a soundless scream. The other faces stirred, eyes opening across the wall to fix Hawk with the same unblinking look of agonised despair. Hawk's stomach lurched as he realized they were all still alive, pinned up and endlessly suffering.

Whatever happened, Hawk swore he'd see Grimm brought to justice for this, at least.

"Isobel, get over here, fast."

Fisher ran quickly to join him, sword in hand, and stared numbly at the writhing faces on the wall. "My God, Hawk. What kind of bastard . . . We've got to do something. We can't leave them like this."

"No, we can't. Try the suppressor stone. Maybe it'll cancel out the magic that's keeping them alive."

Fisher nodded, and ran the stone slowly over the staring faces. One by one the eyes closed and did not open again. The life went out of the faces, and soon they were nothing more than empty masks, pinned to a wall. At rest, at last. Fisher touched a few of them tentatively, but they didn't respond. The skin was soft, but already cooling. Just to be sure, Hawk had her run the suppressor stone over the dissected cat as well.

They took turns examining the papers Fisher had found in Grimm's desk. They seemed to be records of services Grimm had provided in the past, but no names were ever mentioned, only initials. It was mostly cosmetic sorcery, though some of the more bizarre requests made Hawk blink. There was no accounting for taste. But interesting though the documents were, there was nothing in them to tie Grimm in with the spy Fenris. Or at least, nothing Hawk could recognize. He threw the papers back onto the desk, and looked frustratedly around him.

"We're not going to find anything here. He's too careful, too meticulous. Probably keeps the important information locked up in his head."

"So let the Guard sorcerers get it out of him," said Fisher. "Let them earn their money for a change."

There was a low groan from behind them, and they looked quickly round. At the other end of the room the sorcerer Grimm was rising unsteadily to his feet. He shook his head once to clear it, and then his gaze fell on Hawk and Fisher and his face darkened. He smiled slowly, removed his robe and threw it to one side. Ropes of muscle bulged suddenly across his bare chest and shoulders, pushing out the taut skin. Hawk and Fisher watched transfixed as the sorcerer changed. His body stretched and swelled, impossible muscles crawling over an inhumanly magnified frame. His face trembled, the features shifting grotesquely as his inner rage expressed itself in distorted flesh and bone. His eyes became featureless black pools, and sharp jagged teeth distorted the shape of his mouth. Grimm padded slowly forward, his crooked hands growing razored claws.

"I think we may have a problem here," said Hawk, taking a firm hold on his axe.

"You always did have a gift for understatement," said Fisher. "What the hell's happening to him?"

"From the look of it, I'd say the sorcerer wasn't averse to sampling his own wares. He's got to the stage where he can shapechange at will."

"You know, this strikes me as a good time to get the hell out of here and yell for reinforcements."

"We can't. He's between us and the nearest door. We're going to have to stop him ourselves."

"Oh, great. How?"

"I'm thinking!"

Grimm lurched forward, his jaws snapping shut like a steel trap. There was no longer anything human in his face. Hawk and Fisher quickly separated, to attack him from different sides, and each of the sorcerer's eyes crawled to different positions on his head so that he could watch both Guards at once. Hawk darted in and cut at Grimm with his axe. The heavy steel head sheared through the sorcerer's waist and out again, but no blood flew. The wound closed immediately, the unnatural flesh flowing seamlessly back together again. Fisher cut at Grimm from the other side, to no better effect. The sorcerer reached for Hawk with a gnarled, clawed hand. Hawk quickly retreated, but the hand just kept coming after him as the arm stretched to an impossible length.

"The stone!" yelled Hawk, backing frantically away. "Try the suppressor stone on him!"

"I've already tried that! It doesn't seem to affect him!"

"Well, keep trying!" Hawk threw himself to one side and the clawing hand dug deep furrows in the wall behind him. He darted behind the writing desk. Grimm demolished it with one blow of a spiked arm. Hawk looked quickly round the room, checking for possible escape routes. Fisher clutched the suppressor stone in her hand, muttering the activating phrase over and over again. The stone suddenly flared with light, bright and dazzling, burning her hand with sudden heat. Fisher threw the stone straight at the sorcerer's misshapen face. He snatched it out of midair and looked at it curiously. The stone exploded, ripping the sorcerer's head from his body and shattering every window in the room.

For a long moment there was silence, broken only by soft settling sounds as debris from the explosion pattered to the floor. Hawk and Fisher got slowly to their feet, brushing dust from their clothes. Where the hideous creature had been, lay a headless human body. Hawk shook his head gingerly, trying to shift the ringing in his ears. Fisher put an arm round his shoulders, and they leaned companionably together for a moment.

"We didn't do too well with this one, did we, Hawk?"

"You could say that. Fenris has escaped, with a new face and body. The one man who could have helped us find him is now dead. And on top of all that, we've lost our suppressor stone. Some days you just shouldn't get out of bed."

"Well," said Fisher, "at least this time they can't blame us for being impulsive." Hawk looked at her. Fisher gestured at Grimm's body. "After all, he's the one who lost his head."

2

Fenris Gone to Ground

The cleanup squad finally made its appearance, with a meat wagon not far behind. Two Guard Constables chalked a rough outline round the headless body, and made laborious notes about the state of the corpse. The forensic sorcerer waited impatiently for them to finish, already in a foul mood at being dragged from his bed so early in the morning. Hawk and Fisher leant against a wall together, drinking the late sorcerer's wine and trying to put together some kind of report that wouldn't get them both busted down to Constable, or beyond.

The two Constables unhurriedly compared notes, and then got out of the way so that the forensic sorcerer could do his stuff. He glared venomously at them, then knelt down by the body and rolled up his sleeves. Hawk and Fisher looked at each other and unanimously decided this might be a good time to get some fresh air. On-the-spot autopsies tended to be thorough, but messy. Hawk drained the last of the wine from the bottle he and Fisher had been passing back and forth, and his lips thinned away from the dregs. It had been a piss-poor vintage, but the sourness suited his mood. No matter what kind of report he and Fisher eventually handed in, he had no doubt they were both in real trouble.

They left Grimm's quarters and clattered down the exterior stairway to the street below. The meat wagon's horses tossed their heads and snorted loudly, their breath steaming on the chill air. Hawk looked away. Reminders of his own mortality made him uncomfortable. Strange lights flared in the windows above as the forensic sorcerer set about dismantling Grimm's remaining wards and shields, and defusing any booby traps that hadn't yet been triggered. Fisher hugged herself as a cold wind swept by.

"I can't help thinking we're missing something, Hawk. We know why Fenris came here; to get a new face. But how did Grimm get involved with Fenris in the first place? He had a nice little racket going here. Judging by the records we found, he was already making more money than he knew what to do with. So why risk it all, by dealing with a traitor? He didn't need the money, and there's nothing in his file to suggest he was at all political."

"Maybe he just liked the excitement, the intrigue," said Hawk. "He wouldn't be the first fool to be seduced by dreams of making history, of playing with the real shakers and movers. Or maybe he just had some kind of grudge against the Council, and saw this as his chance for revenge. I've known stranger motives. Doesn't make much difference now, anyway. The man is dead, and our case died with him. Odds are we'll never find out what it was all about."

The low, steady clamour of a brass bell filled both their heads as the Guard communications sorcerer made contact. Hawk shook his head gingerly as the deep ringing sound faded away. "I think I preferred it when he used the gong. That bloody bell goes right through me." He broke off as the bell gave way to the rasping voice of the communications sorcerer.

Captains Hawk and Fisher are to report to Commander Dubois at Guard Headquarters immediately. This instruction has top priority. All other orders are rescinded.

Hawk and Fisher waited a moment to see if there was any more, and then looked at each other. "Didn't take long for the news to reach our superiors, did it?" said Hawk.

Fisher shrugged. "Haven loves bad news. And you can bet there were people lining up for the chance to drop us in it. We've always been too honest to be popular."

"What the hell," said Hawk. "We've weathered worse storms than this."

"Right," said Fisher. "Just keep our heads down, and it'll all blow over."

"You really believe that?"

"No. How about you?"

"No. Even so, Dubois had better not shout at me," said Hawk firmly. "I'm not in the mood to be shouted at. In fact, if he raises his voice to me I think I'll hit him somewhere low and painful."

"How is that going to help us?"

"It couldn't hurt."

"True."

Hawk and Fisher had barely walked through the front door at Guard Headquarters when a Constable appeared, seemingly from nowhere, and insisted on escorting them straight to Dubois' office. Other Guards avoided Hawk's and Fisher's eyes as they made their way through the Headquarters building. Word had got around and no one wanted to risk guilt by association. Hawk smiled humourlessly, and let his hand drift down to the axe at his side. He glanced across at Fisher, and saw that her hand was already resting on the pommel of her sword.

The Constable brought them to Dubois' office and knocked briskly on the door. There was barely a pause before the Commander's voice summoned them in. The Constable opened the door, and stood back for Hawk and Fisher to enter. Hawk strolled casually in, Fisher at his side. The door shut behind them. Hawk listened carefully, but didn't hear any sound of the Constable departing. Now, that was interesting. It meant that the man was still there. Presumably on guard to keep people out . . . or in. Hawk smiled inwardly as he and Fisher bowed formally to Commander Dubois. If he and Fisher decided it was in their best interests to leave in a hurry, it would take a lot more than one Guard Constable to stop them.

Dubois glared at Hawk and Fisher from behind his desk and sniffed disgustedly. "Gods, you're a mess. I've seen beggars in the Devil's Hook who looked more presentable than you two do right now. You're a disgrace to your uniform.''

Hawk looked down at himself, and had to admit the Commander had a point. His clothes were badly torn and soaked with blood from the various fights he'd got involved in that evening. A quick glance at Fisher revealed she hadn't fared any better. Her furs were stained and matted from the garbage she'd fallen in outside Madam Zara's. And what with all the exertions of the evening, the fact was they both smelled pretty bad. Hawk had a sudden intense desire to stand downwind of himself. He looked back at Dubois, and put on his best innocent face. Dubois glared at him even harder. The complete lack of hair on his head somehow made his scowl all the more impressive.

''And you've lost your cloak again, Hawk! What happened this time? Someone sneak up behind you and steal it while you weren't looking? Where the hell is your cloak?''

Hawk had to stop and think, so Fisher quickly answered for him. ''It's pinned to a wall in a spiritualist's house.''

Dubois winced. ''I'm not even going to ask you what you were doing at a spiritualist's. I don't think my nerves could stand it. Do you realize, Hawk, you go through more new cloaks in a year than most Guards use up in a lifetime's service to the city? Do you know how much those cloaks cost?''

''Yes,'' said Hawk. ''Because you always deduct the cost from my wages.''

''Damn right!'' said Dubois. ''You're not screwing up my budget for the year. Perhaps you would also like to explain why you failed to turn in your suppressor stone to the Armoury, as ordered.''

''Would that help to get us off the hook?'' said Hawk.

''Not in the least.''

''Then I don't think I'll bother.''

Fisher butted in quickly as Dubois' face darkened. ''Be fair; it saved both our arses tonight. If the stone hadn't blown up in Grimm's face when it did, we might both have been killed.''

"I could live with that," said Dubois.

He picked up a sheet of paper from his desk and frowned at it. Hawk studied the Commander's bowed head thoughtfully. Something was going on. Dubois should be tearing strips off them for letting Fenris get away, not carping about their appearance, or niggling over lost cloaks and the illegal use of a suppressor stone. Dubois had never made any secret of the fact that he didn't approve of Hawk and Fisher's methods, and was usually only too happy to find something about their work he could criticize. The Fenris debacle should have been just what he need to bust them down to Constable, or worse. Instead, he hadn't even mentioned the spy. If he hadn't known better, Hawk would have sworn Dubois was trying to avoid telling them something unpleasant.

Hawk's mind raced furiously. Maybe the Council had found out about Fenris getting away, and had decided to blame everything on the two Guards. It wouldn't be too hard for the Council to make out a case of treason against them. They could claim the Guards had deliberately let the spy escape, and then killed Grimm to cover their tracks. Hawk forced himself to calm down. It needn't be that bad. It could be that Dubois just had some really nasty job lined up for them, as penance for failing to bring in Fenris. Now, that was much more likely. Hawk began to relax a little. Whatever it was, he and Fisher could handle it. After five years working the Northside they could handle anything.

Dubois carefully put down the piece of paper, tapped it with his fingers a few times, and then looked up at Hawk and Fisher. "For once in your lives, you've struck it lucky. We know where Fenris is. The Council circle of sorcerers knew that Grimm was somehow involved with the traitors, and kept an unobtrusive watch on him. So when Fenris did a runner with his new face, they were able to follow him magically, all the way to his new hiding place."

"Wait a minute," said Fisher. "If we know where he is, why can't we just walk right in and grab him?"

"Unfortunately, it's not that simple."

"Somehow I didn't think it would be," said Hawk.

Dubois sniffed. "Fenris has gone to ground at Tower MacNeil, just outside the city wall. That much the sorcerers are certain of. But it seems our man has some sorcerous protection of his own, presumably supplied by his superiors. Our people couldn't get close enough to see what his new face looks like."

"No problem," said Hawk. "We burst in there, arrest everyone, and sort out which is Fenris later."

"I thought you'd come up with something like that," said Dubois. "Don't even think about it. The MacNeils are one of the oldest and most respected Families in Haven. We don't dare touch them. If it should turn out one of the MacNeils was the traitor, it would be a major scandal. We have very explicit orders to avoid any such thing. And that, Gods help us, is where you come in."

"All right," said Fisher, "I'll bite. Why us?"

"Well, thanks to you and your partner's incompetence, what description we did have of Fenris is now obsolete. But at least you two have met the man in person. There's always the chance you'll recognize some mannerism or habit that'll give him away. So you are going in there after him, suitably disguised. Your job is to identify Fenris, and get him out of the Tower without anyone else catching on. It's not much of a plan, so the fact that we're going ahead with it will give you some idea of how desperate we are. Any questions so far?"

"Yeah," said Hawk. "What kind of place is Tower MacNeil?"

"Home to the MacNeils for fourteen generations. Protected by old sorcery and one of Haven's finest security firms. The head of the Family, Duncan MacNeil, died last month. Which means, luckily for us, that things are in something of a turmoil at the moment. Duncan's son Jamie is to be the new head of the Family, the MacNeil, as he's called. And, as is customary, all living members of the Family will be gathering at Tower MacNeil to pay their respects to the new head, and jockey for positions of influence and power. Nothing like a Family funeral to bring out the vultures. Fenris will presumably be trying to pass himself off as one of the more remote cousins. Which is how we're going to get you in.''

Hawk and Fisher looked at each other.

''Wait a minute,'' said Hawk. ''You mean we're going to be masquerading as Quality?''

''Got it in one,'' said Dubois. ''What's the matter? Don't you think you can do it?''

''That's not the point,'' said Fisher. ''The last I heard, passing yourself off as Quality was still punishable by death. Is that being waived in our case?''

''No,'' said Dubois. ''Whatever the outcome, officially you were never there. If you do get caught, we'll disclaim all knowledge of you. This is a very delicate situation.''

Hawk thought for a moment. ''Is this a volunteer situation?''

''Yes,'' said Dubois. ''I volunteered you. Given the alternatives, I wouldn't argue if I were you.''

Fisher looked at him steadily. ''We don't like being pressured, Dubois. We don't like it at all.''

Dubois fought down an urge to shrink back in his chair as a sudden chill ran through him. Without moving a muscle, Hawk and Fisher had suddenly become dangerous. An air of menace and imminent violence filled the tiny office, as though a slumbering wolf had suddenly awakened and shown its teeth. Dubois paled slightly, but didn't flinch.

''Renegade Guards tend to have very short life spans,'' he said evenly. ''If anything was to happen to me, you wouldn't even make it to the city gates.''

Hawk smiled. ''You might be right, Dubois. But I wouldn't count on it if I were you. We've faced worse odds in the past. We'll do your dirty work for you, this time. I think we owe it to the Council, for letting Fenris get away from us. But if you ever try to pressure us like this again, Dubois, I'll kill you. Believe it.''

Dubois met Hawk's cold stare for a moment, and then looked away. When he looked back, Hawk and Fisher were just Guards again. The air of violence was gone, as though it had never been. For the first time, Dubois understood how they'd gained their reputation. He got to his feet and cleared his throat carefully. He didn't want to sound nervous or uncertain. "Let's go. We've got just under two hours to turn the pair of you into regular young flowers of the aristocracy and deliver you to Tower MacNeil."

"No problem," said Hawk. "We can be as aristocratic as the next man, if pushed."

"Right," said Fisher, with an impeccable upper-class accent. "All we have to do is act arrogant and obnoxious at all times, and remember not to blow our noses on our sleeves without crooking our little fingers. What could go wrong?"

Dubois swallowed hard, but said nothing. There were times when mere words seemed inadequate.

He hustled them out of his office and through the bustling corridors to an anonymous file room safely out of everyone's way. He ushered them in, and then locked the door behind them. A Guard medical sorcerer rose quickly to his feet, nodded stiffly to the two Guards and looked enquiringly at Dubois. The Commander nodded, and the sorcerer shrugged. He was a dark and intense-looking man in his early forties, with a professional smile and large, powerful hands. He was overdressed in a dark, formal way, as though he were about to attend a funeral. Hawk looked at him suspiciously. He didn't trust Haven doctors. They seemed to believe in suppositories for everything, from warts to deafness. He started to turn to Dubois, but Fisher beat him to it.

"What's the doctor doing here? We're not sick."

"This is Wulfgang. You can trust him completely."

"Why?" said Hawk. "You got something on him too?"

"Wulfgang specializes in shapechange magic, in a minor way," said Dubois. "Since you both have something of a reputation in Haven, we can't have you walking into Tower MacNeil with your own faces, can we? Wulfgang will give you new faces, which won't be recognized."

Hawk scowled at the sorcerer. "I'm not feeling too fond of flesh-sculptors right now. What's wrong with a good old-fashioned illusion spell?"

Dubois sighed impatiently. "Tower MacNeil, like most Quality households, has security spells to show up such things. The Families take their security very seriously. The shapechange won't register because the spell will have finished its work long before you get there. After you return, with your mission successfully completed, we'll give you your own faces back."

"And if we don't succeed?" said Hawk.

Dubois smiled coldly. "You screw up in Tower MacNeil, Hawk, and you won't be coming back. Now, stop holding things up, and let the sorcerer get to work on you. We're running out of time."

Hawk and Fisher looked at each other, and then sat down on the chairs Wulfgang indicated. The sorcerer smiled reassuringly and ran his hands through a series of practised gestures, muttering under his breath as he did so. A gradual feeling of pressure filled the room, and Hawk's skin crawled as static moved in his hair. The pressure peaked uncomfortably, and then vanished as the sorcerer made a final, decisive gesture. Hawk waited a moment, and then looked down at his hands. They still looked the same to him. He looked across at Fisher, and she looked the same too. He looked back at the sorcerer Wulfgang, who was staring dumbfounded at the two Guards.

"Why isn't anything happening?" demanded Dubois.

"I don't know!" snapped Wulfgang. "I can't understand it; the spell just seemed to slide off them." A sudden thought struck him, and he glared at Hawk. "Are you still carrying your suppressor stone?"

"No, he isn't," said Dubois. "And don't ask what happened to it. That's confidential."

Wulfgang frowned thoughtfully. "There's nothing wrong with the spell, they're not shielded, so what . . . ? Wait a minute. Have you two ever been exposed to Wild Magic?"

"What's that got to do with anything?" said Dubois.

"There's a big difference between the High Magic that most sorcerers use, and the much rarer Wild Magic," said Wulfgang patiently. "High Magic manipulates aspects of the real world; Wild Magic changes reality itself. So if your people have been exposed to Wild Magic . . ."

"We have," said Hawk. "We were up North when the Blue Moon rose."

Dubois and Wulfgang stared at the two Guards almost respectfully. "You were there, during the long night?" said Dubois.

"We were there," said Fisher. "And no, we don't want to talk about it."

"That's why my spell won't work on them," said Wulfgang. "If they were exposed to the Blue Moon's influence, it'll take more than a simple shapechange spell to affect them. I'm sorry, Commander. There's nothing I can do."

Dubois sighed. "I might have known you two were going to be trouble. All right. Thank you, Wulfgang. That will be all. The wardrobe mistress should have arrived by now; perhaps you'd be good enough to ask her to step in here on your way out. And Wulfgang, remember: This meeting never took place. You were never here."

"Of course," said the sorcerer. He bowed politely to Hawk and Fisher, and waited patiently for Dubois to unlock the door so he could leave. Dubois locked the door again after he'd gone.

"While we're waiting," said Hawk, "there's a few things I'd like to get clear. In particular, why Fenris chose Tower MacNeil as his hiding place. Surely among so many Quality he'd be bound to give himself away sooner or later."

Dubois pursed his lips. "We have reason to believe Fenris may be of the Quality," he said carefully. "So he'd have no problem passing himself off as a distant MacNeil cousin."

"Why the hell would one of the Quality want to act as a spy?" said Hawk. "Most spies work strictly for cash, or occasionally political gain. If there's one thing the Quality aren't short of, it's money, and most of them don't give a damn about politics. So what happened to turn Fenris into an agent for a foreign power?"

"If we knew that, we'd know who he was," said Dubois. "Can you at least tell us something about the information

he's stolen?'' said Fisher. "That might help when it comes
to identifying him.''

"I can't tell you anything,'' said Dubois flatly. "That's
being handled on a strictly need-to-know basis. Even I
haven't been told. But it must be pretty damned important
to have got everyone running round in circles like this. You
wouldn't believe the pressure that's been coming down from
Above. Let me put it this way: Under no circumstances is
the spy Fenris to be allowed to escape from Tower MacNeil.
If he tries, you're to stop him, whatever it takes.''

"You mean kill him?'' said Fisher.

"Whatever it takes,'' said Dubois.

Hawk smiled sourly. "In other words, it's up to us
whether or not we kill a member of the Quality. But if
anything goes wrong afterwards, everyone will swear blind
we were never given any such order. Right?''

"Got it in one,'' said Dubois. "You have a natural gift
for politics, Hawk.''

They sat in silence for a while, each thinking their own
separate thoughts. There was a knock at the door. Dubois
went over and quietly asked who it was. On getting a sat-
isfactory answer, he unlocked the door. But he still stood
well back as it opened, one hand resting on his sword till
he saw the newcomer was alone. The wardrobe mistress
bustled in, in a hurry as usual. Mistress Melanie was tall
and scrawny, with a sharp-boned face and a wild frizz of
dark curly hair barely restrained by a leather headband. She
was one of those people who had so much nervous energy
she made everyone else feel tired just looking at her.

"Are they ready?'' she said sharply to Dubois, not even
bothering to look at Hawk and Fisher.

Dubois nodded briskly. "The shapechange didn't take.
We'll have to rely on standard disguise techniques. Do what
you can with them.''

Mistress Melanie made a short tutting sound and glared
at the two Guards. "As if we weren't already running behind
schedule. All right. Follow me and don't dawdle.''

And with that, she disappeared back out the door while

her words were still ringing on the air. Hawk and Fisher hurried after her.

A short footrace later, they ended up in the wardrobe department. Hawk had never been there before and looked around with interest. Hundreds of costumes hung in neat rows on wire hangers—everything from the latest Quality fashions to a filthy ragpicker's outfit. A great deal of the Guard's work had to be done undercover; inevitable in a city like Haven, where no one shared confidences unless they had to and absolutely no one spoke to the authorities. Unless there was money in it. Half the Guard's annual budget went to information-gathering, a fact which never failed to infuriate the more penny-pinching members of the Council.

Mistress Melanie sat Hawk and Fisher down in front of the makeup mirrors and studied them thoughtfully. "Yes," she said finally, drawing out the word till it sounded more like *no*, "The scars are going to be a problem, but a good coat of makeup should cover them. No one'll be able to tell, even at close quarters, but don't let anyone kiss you."

"I hadn't planned on it," said Hawk.

Mistress Melanie sniffed. "We're going to have to do something about that eye, of course. A patch is out of the question." She looked hard at Hawk's single eye for a moment, then opened a small lacquered box and rummaged around inside it, finally producing a single glass eye. "Try this."

"No," said Hawk flatly. "Forget it. I hate the damned things."

"I can assure you, you'll find it a perfect match," said Mistress Melanie frostily.

"I said no!"

"Be reasonable, Hawk," said Fisher. "You can't wear your patch. Any member of the Quality who suffered that kind of injury would have it put right at once with a shape-change spell. And since you can't do that, you'll have to use the glass eye. It won't be for long."

Hawk growled something indistinct, and accepted the

glass eye with bad grace. He scowled at it for a moment, then took off his patch, put it to one side, and gingerly eased the glass eye into the empty socket. He blinked experimentally a few times, and then glared into the mirror. "Hate wearing a glass eye," he growled. "Makes my face ache."

Fisher looked over his shoulder into the mirror. "She's right, Hawk; they're a perfect match. No one will be able to tell it isn't real."

Hawk sniffed loudly, unimpressed. Mistress Melanie produced a set of clothes for each of them, and thrust them unceremoniously into Hawk and Fisher's arms. "Try these for size. They're based on the statistics in your official records, but I've had to make some allowances. From the look of you, you've both put on some weight since then. Come on, get a move on; I've got to know if I have to make more alterations, and we've still got your makeup to do."

Hawk looked at her and raised an eyebrow meaningfully. Mistress Melanie's mouth twitched. "I'll wait outside while you change. Call me if you have any problems."

She left, closing the door firmly behind her. Hawk took his first good look at his new clothes, and his heart sank. The latest male fashion for the Quality still consisted of tightly cut trousers, a padded jerkin with a chin-high collar, and knee-length leather boots. Plus some rather utilitarian long underwear. The jerkin and trousers were both navy blue with gold thread trim. The military look was *in* this Season. He looked across at Fisher, and smiled as he saw she was even less enchanted with her new clothes. There was a long flowing gown of lilac blue with frothy lace trim, a great deal of frilly underwear, a formidable-looking corset, and a pair of fashionable shoes that looked hideously uncomfortable. Fisher picked up the corset with a thumb and forefinger and held it out at arm's length, studying it dubiously.

"Look on the bright side," said Hawk. "At least there isn't a bustle."

"Do we really have to do this, Hawk?" said Fisher.

"Well, we could fight our way out of here, and make a run for it."

"Don't tempt me." Fisher sighed heavily, and began stripping off her furs. "The things I do in the line of duty . . ."

It took them the best part of half an hour to climb into their new clothes. There were endless buttons and hooks and eyes, and they all had to be done up in just the right order. Hawk could only just get into the trousers. Even with Mistress Melanie's allowances for his somewhat expanded waistline, it was a very tight fit. Fisher had even more trouble with the corset. Hawk ended up having to put a knee in the middle of her back while he pulled the cords tight. Fisher's language became increasingly awful, until finally she was forced to give up from lack of breath. Finally, the ordeal was over, and they stood together before a full-length mirror, judging the effect.

Despite everything, Hawk had to admit they looked the part. Before them in the mirror stood a gentleman and young lady of the Quality, dressed impeccably in the latest finery. Hawk looked splendid and striking, though the scars on his face still gave him a sinister air, and Fisher looked absolutely stunning. The corset had given her a magnificent hourglass figure, and the long gown made her look even taller. She winked at Hawk coquettishly over her paper fan, and they both laughed.

"Been a long time since we looked this good," said Hawk finally.

"A long time," said Fisher.

Mistress Melanie knocked loudly, and swept in without waiting for an answer. She looked them both up and down, and nodded curtly. "You'll do. Now let's see what we can achieve with a little makeup."

Another half hour passed before the wardrobe mistress allowed Hawk and Fisher to look into a mirror again, and what they saw kept them silent for a long moment. Their skin was now fashionably pale instead of their usual tan. Fisher's face had been expertly made up with rouge and eye shadow, taking the edge off the harsh lines, and softening the aggressive chin. Her long blond hair had been piled up on top of her head in a complicated design. Hawk's face had changed completely; with the patch gone and the scars hidden under makeup he looked ten years younger, and somehow more at peace with himself and the world. Fisher looked at him and smiled tenderly.

"I often wondered what you looked like, before the scars."

"Well?" said Hawk awkwardly. "What do you think?"

"I think you look very handsome, my love. But then, I always did."

Hawk leant forward to kiss her, and Mistress Melanie yelled at him. "No touching till the makeup's set! I don't want to have to fix her face all over again!"

Hawk and Fisher shared a wry smile. There was a loud knocking at the door.

"Are you two decent?" called Commander Dubois from outside.

"Near as we ever get," said Hawk loudly, and nodded for Mistress Melanie to let the Commander in. Hawk and Fisher struck carefully aristocratic poses and stared haughtily at Dubois as he came in. He walked slowly over to them, and looked from one to the other and back again.

"I'm . . . impressed," he said finally. "You might just bring this off after all. I wish we had time to give you a full briefing on how to behave, all the little tricks of etiquette and the like, but we're way behind schedule as it is."

"Don't worry," said Hawk. "We know which fork to use, and which way to pass the port. We've been around."

"Right," said Fisher. "You'd be surprised."

"Yeah, well," said Dubois. "We've worked out a rough background for you. You're going to be remote country cousins of the MacNeils; a brother and sister from the wilds of Lower Markham. That's way out on the Eastern border, so no one should be able to trip you up on local details. Make up anything you like; they won't know the difference. But keep it simple. You don't want to end up contradicting each other. Also, they'll expect a certain amount of gaucherie and unfamiliarity with the latest styles, so that should help excuse any foul-ups you do make. Now then, you're going to have to get used to your new names. Captain Fisher can use her given name of Isobel. That's quite a fashionable name at the moment. But we don't seem to have a given name on the files for you, Captain Hawk.''

"There isn't one. I'm just Hawk."

"You only have the one name?"

"I've had others. But I'm just Hawk now."

"Be that as it may," said Dubois, in the tone of someone determined not to ask questions he's sure he wouldn't like the answers to. "As far as you're concerned, from now on you're Richard MacNeil. Got it?"

"Richard . . ." said Hawk. "Yeah. I can live with that."

"I'm so pleased," said Dubois. "One last thing: Leave your axe here. We'll supply you with a standard duelling sword. And Captain Fisher will have to go unarmed, of course. No young lady of the Quality would wear a sword. It simply isn't done.''

Hawk and Fisher looked at each other.

"No axe."

"No sword."

"Tight trousers."

"And a bloody corset."

They looked hard at Dubois. "We want a bonus," said Hawk flatly.

"In cash," said Fisher.

"In our hands, before we go."

"I can arrange that," said Dubois.

Hawk looked at Fisher. "They must really be desperate."

"Maybe we should hit them for overtime while we're at it," said Fisher.

"Don't push your luck," said Dubois.

3

Ghosts and Memories

Haven was an old city, but the dark and brooding cliffs that overlooked it were older still. Huge and forbidding, they rose out of the restless sea like grim, watchful guardians, protecting Haven on three sides from the raging storms that swept in off the sea. The waves pounded endlessly at the jagged spurs of rock, throwing spray high into the wind even on the calmest of days. Tower MacNeil stood firm and unyielding on an outcropping of dark basalt that jutted from the cliff face like a clenched fist against the encroaching sea.

The Tower was tall and elegant, built entirely from the local white stone, with its distinctive pearly sheen. Its lines were clean and functional, the wide glass windows its only concession to comfort and luxury. It stood five stories tall, surmounted by open crenellated battlements. Down the centuries, Tower MacNeil had defied both time and the elements, as well as countless enemy attacks. Often scarred, and as often restored, it had never once fallen to its adversaries. Brilliant engineering and subtle sorceries maintained the Tower, as it maintained and protected the Family who dwelt within.

But like the cliffs on which it stood, and the dark city it overlooked, Tower MacNeil had its grim and bloody secrets.

Within the Tower, something had stirred; something strange and awful, free of its chains at last.

Hawk trudged up the single narrow path, his cloak pulled tightly about him, his head bowed against the gusting wind. This high up on the cliffs the wind blew hard and bitter cold. The wild grasses seemed permanentely flattened by the weather, and nothing else grew about him for as far as he could see. Hawk wasn't surprised, given the force of the winds. Anything that dared thrust its head above the ground was probably ripped out by the roots for its impertinence. He raised his head slightly, and scowled as he saw Fisher waiting for him some way ahead, standing on the edge of the cliff and looking out to sea. He took a few deep breaths, fighting to get his breathing back to normal before he joined her. The long steep trail had winded him, but he didn't want her to know that. She'd only make pointed comments about his being out of condition and put him on another diet. Hawk hated diets. Why did everything that was good for you have to taste so bloody bland?

He crossed over to stand beside Fisher on the cliff edge, careful to keep a respectful distance between him and the crumbling stone brink. The wind tugged at his hair and drew tears from his eyes. Fisher nodded at him happily, and indicated the view with a sweeping wave of her arm. Hawk had to admit it was pretty breathtaking. Far below, waves pounded the rocks with unrelenting fury, falling reluctantly back in streams of froth and spume. The choppy sea stretched away to the horizon in endless shades of blue and green and grey, empty of sails for once. Winter was closing in, and ships now were few and far between. The steely blue sky was clear of clouds for the moment, thanks to the city weather wizards, and gulls hung on the air like drifting shadows, tossed here and there by the gusting wind. Their mournful keening was all that broke the morning quiet, save for the distant crash of breakers down below.

"Listen to the sea and the gulls," said Fisher. "So wild, so free. We really should get out here more often, Hawk."

"Maybe we will, come the summer. And you'd better

call me Richard from now on, even when there's no one around. We don't want to get caught out on something that simple.''

"Sure. Why did we have to be brother and sister? Why couldn't we be husband and wife?"

"Beats me. Maybe we're supposed to get information out of people by romancing them."

Fisher wrinkled her nose. "Not really our style, that."

"True."

"I never get tired of looking at the sea. I never even saw the ocean before we left the North."

"I like the view too, Isobel, but we can't stay here. We have a job to do, and time is pressing."

"I know. It's just that we never seem to have any time to ourselves these days."

"When did we ever?"

"True. Let's go."

They turned away from the cliff edge and made their way back through the grass to the narrow stony trail. The Tower loomed ahead of them, straight and uncompromising against the skyline, silent and enigmatic. Its height made it look deceptively slim until you got close enough to realize just how huge the Tower really was. Hawk thought for a moment on how backbreaking it must have been, hauling building stone up the cliffs to this spot, and then decided firmly that he wasn't going to think about it anymore. Just trying to visualize the logistics was enough to make his head ache. He realized Fisher was staring at the Tower too, and deliberately quickened his step.

"Come on, Isobel," he said briskly. "There's no telling how long Fenris will stay put in the Tower. If he decides to leave before we can get there to stop him, Dubois will have our heads. Probably literally."

"I don't know why Fenris didn't just keep running," said Fisher, picking up the pace. "I would have. What made him think he'd be safe here?"

"The longer he stayed in the open, the more likely it was he'd be spotted," said Hawk. "And the Tower's a good place to go to ground. It's within easy reach of the city but out of everyone's thoughts. I wouldn't have thought to look for him here. If it hadn't been for the Council's sorcerers, he'd have probably got away with it. And let's face it. If worst came to worst, and for some reason the MacNeils decided not to hand him over, we'd have one hell of a job getting him out of the Tower. You'd need an army and every sorcerer in the city to breach those walls, by all accounts. No, my guess is Fenris is probably biding his time in there, looking over his shoulder a lot and waiting for one of his own people to contact him with a safe route out of the Low Kingdoms. Assuming someone hasn't already done so.''

"I still haven't figured out what we're going to do once we're inside the Tower," said Fisher. "I mean, we've no idea what he looks like now. He could be anybody. He could be passing himself off as an out-of-town MacNeil cousin, like us, or a friend of one, or a newly hired servant, or . . . Hell, I don't know. The man's a spy, after all; he's used to pretending to be someone he isn't. How are we going to trip up someone like that? This case is a mess, and we've barely even started yet. Do you think we're going to be able to recognize him?''

"Not a hope," said Hawk. "If I had to fight him again I might recognize his style, but I'm damned if I'm going to go round challenging everyone to a duel. Especially without my axe. Have you seen this stupid sword they've given me? One good parry and it'll snap in half. I'd be better off sneaking up behind my opponent and clubbing him to death with the hilt.''

"So what are we going to do?''

"Same as usual, lass. Ask lots of questions, keep our eyes open, and hopefully make enough of a nuisance of ourselves that the killer will do something stupid to try and shut us up.''

"Great," said Fisher. "I just love being a target.''

They both fell silent as they finally drew near the Tower MacNeil. The large, squarish front door was a different shade of white from the surrounding stonework, and Hawk felt a sudden, unsettling thrill go through him as he realized the door had been carved from a single huge slab of polished ivory. He tried to visualize the size of the whale that could donate such a bone, and quickly decided he'd rather not know. He tugged briskly at the bell pull, and then he and Fisher took turns using the black iron boot-scraper. They were Quality now, and had to keep up appearances.

The door swung smoothly open on well-oiled counter-weights, revealing a medium-height, heavyset man in his mid-forties, wearing the slightly outdated formal wear that was the accepted hallmark of the Haven butler. He had dark, lifeless hair, a flat immobile face that might have been carved from stone, and a general air of gloomy efficiency for which the long black frock coat was the perfect finishing touch. He bowed formally to Hawk and Fisher, each bow nicely calculated to the inch to show respect for his betters whilst reminding them that as butler of the household he was a force to be reckoned with in his own right. It was a masterful performance. Hawk felt like applauding.

"I am Richard MacNeil of Lower Markham," he said gravely. "This is my sister, Isobel. We've come to pay our respects to the new head of the Family."

"Of course, sir and madam. I am Greaves, butler of Tower MacNeil. Please come in."

He stood back to allow them to enter. He seemed faintly disapproving, possibly because they came from a backwater like Lower Markham, but most likely because butlers always seemed faintly disapproving. Hawk suspected it was part of the job description. He strolled into the hallway as though he owned the place, with Isobel on his arm, smiling de-murely. The smile didn't suit her, but Hawk admired the effort that had gone into it. Greaves closed the door behind them, and Hawk's ears pricked up as he heard the sound of heavy bolts being thrown home. It could be that the Tower MacNeil household was routinely security-minded . . . or it could be that right now they had reason to be. He took off his cloak, and found the butler already there waiting to receive it. Fisher handed Greaves her cloak, and raised a painted eyebrow enquiringly.

"Are you the only staff here, Greaves? Surely it's not a

butler's place to take the cloaks from guests. Don't you have any maids under you?''

Greaves's expression didn't alter in the least as he arranged the cloaks neatly on the wall by the door. "Alas, madam, I'm afraid Tower MacNeil is extremely short staffed at present. Normally we have a staff of twenty-two, but everyone else left some time ago.''

Hawk looked at him sharply. "And why is that?''

"It's not really my place to say, sir. If you and the young lady would care to follow me, I'll take you to the MacNeil himself. I'm sure he will be happy to answer any questions you may have.''

He turned his back on them, politely but firmly, and started off down the hall. Hawk and Fisher exchanged a look behind his back, shrugged pretty much in unison, and followed him. They'd only been in the place a few moments and already they were up to their ears in questions. What the hell could have happened here to drive all the servants out? And since it had happened recently, could it have something to do with Fenris' arrival? The butler worried Hawk as well. The man was being far too calm and pleasant. Most butlers were worse snobs than their masters and would have had coronaries at the mere mention of their doing maids' work. And yet Greaves seemed to be implying he was doing all the servants' work at Tower MacNeil. What kind of hold could keep him at his duty, despite the humiliation?

Hawk shrugged inwardly. Perhaps Greaves was just angling for a larger than usual gratuity when Hawk left. In which case, he was going to be disappointed. Wardrobe might have provided Hawk with aristocratic clothes, but they'd absolutely declined to fill the purse on his belt. He'd had to do that, with his bonus money, and he was damned if he was going to part with one penny more than he absolutely had to.

The butler led Hawk and Fisher down a stylishly appointed passage and ushered them into a large and spacious drawing room. Early morning light streamed through the immaculately polished windows, reflecting brightly from the pure white of the stonework, illuminating the room like a vision of paradise. The whole ceiling was covered with a single delightful piece of art depicting nymphs and shepherds at play. In a romantic and extremely tasteful way, of course. Everywhere there were luxurious chairs and couches, fine displays of wines and spirits, silver trays bearing all kinds of cold food, and every other comfort the mind could imagine. Hawk did his best to look unimpressed.

Standing with his back to the roaring fire was a tall, well-built young man with broad shoulders and a barrel chest. He couldn't have been more than twenty, and his unruly mop of tawny hair made him look even younger. Nevertheless, there was a dignity and strength in his stance, and a composure in his face, that was quietly impressive. Hawk didn't need Greaves to tell him this was their host, Jamie MacNeil. The MacNeil, as he now was. He was dressed all in black, being still in mourning for his father, but the clothes were of the finest cut and impeccably fashionable. He stepped forward as the butler introduced them, and greeted his two cousins warmly, kissing Isobel's hand with style, and shaking Hawk's hand in a grip that was firm without being overbearing. He gestured for the butler to leave them, and Greaves bowed and backed out, closing the door after him. Jamie led Hawk and Fisher over to the drinks cabinet and politely enquired as to their pleasure. He seemed genuinely pleased to see them, and yet somehow preoccupied, as though part of his attention was always somewhere else.

"So good of you to come," he said graciously. "Did you have a good journey?"

"Bearable," said Hawk, accepting his drink with a nod. "We left our belongings in Haven, ghastly place, and came straight here. Though I gather from your butler that we may have arrived at a bad time . . . he said something about all the servants leaving?"

Jamie MacNeil smiled easily, but Hawk could see the effort it took. "Just a minor domestic crisis, but I'm afraid we're all going to have to rough it for the moment. Please accept my apologies, and bear with us. Do feel free to stay for as long as you wish; there are plenty of spare bedrooms, and Haven's inns are notoriously unsafe."

"That's very kind of you," said Hawk.

"Not at all, not at all. I'll just let Greaves know, and he'll prepare rooms for you and your sister."

He reached for the bell pull by the fireplace, but had barely taken hold of it when the door swung open and Greaves entered. Hawk blinked bemusedly at such a quick response, and then smiled slightly as Greaves stepped to one side and two ladies of the Quality swept in, not even deigning to notice the butler's bow. Jamie smiled at them both, a genuine smile full of warmth and affection, and more than a little concern. Hawk sipped his wine thoughtfully as Jamie spoke quietly to the butler. He was beginning to get a bad feeling about Tower MacNeil. Something was going on here; something he was beginning to suspect had nothing to do with the spy Fenris. He took a healthy gulp of his wine, careful to keep his little finger crooked. On the other hand, he could just be getting paranoid. If Jamie MacNeil knew about the spy, then getting rid of a bunch of gossiping servants was a sensible precaution. But according to Greaves, the servants had left some time ago, long before Fenris could have arrived. . . . Hawk quickly put the thought to one side for later consideration as Jamie dismissed the butler and turned to him and Fisher.

"Dear cousins, allow me to present my sister Holly, and my aunt, Katrina Dorimant."

Hawk bowed and the women curtsied, Fisher with more efficiency than grace. Holly MacNeil was a blazing redhead in her late twenties, almost as tall as her brother, but as slightly built as he was broad. Hawk's first thought was that the poor lass could do with a good meal or two. Her pale face was gaunt and strained, though still attractive, her large green eyes giving her an innocent, vulnerable look, like a young fawn suddenly confronted with a pack of wolves. Whatever was going on at Tower MacNeil, it was clear she knew about it too. Like her brother, Holly MacNeil was formally but stylishly dressed in black, which against the paleness of her skin only served to emphasize her frailty.

She offered Hawk a trembling hand, and he had to steady it with his own before he could kiss it. He gave her hand a reassuring squeeze before releasing it, and thought he glimpsed a quick smile. Holly and Fisher embraced each other briefly. There was no warmth in it, and Holly held the contact only as long as convention demanded.

Jamie's aunt, Katrina Dorimant, was a roguishly attractive woman in her mid-forties, with a broad grin and flashing eyes. She wore a long, wine-red gown, and enough jewellery to finance a minor war or two. She was average height, with a tight, compact body and a brisk, captivating manner. She smiled widely at Hawk as he kissed her hand, and her eyes lingered on him for a long moment before she turned to embrace Fisher. Once again the embrace was over almost as soon as it had begun, and the two women exchanged a cool, appraising look before dismissing each other with averted eyes. Hawk hid a smile. Fisher had better keep her guard up. Katrina looked like a scrapper.

"Welcome to Tower MacNeil!" said Katrina brightly. "I'm so glad you're here. We need some new blood to stir things up. The place has been awfully gloomy just lately, though I can't think why. Dear Duncan never approved of sour faces when he was alive, and he certainly wouldn't have expected us to wander around sobbing and beating our breasts just because he's dead."

"You never did believe in tears or regrets, did you, Aunt?" said Holly flatly.

"Certainly not. They make your eyes puffy and give you wrinkles."

"Are you here for the reading of the will?" asked Fisher politely.

"Actually, no, my dear. I'm currently separated from my husband, bad cess to the man, and dear Jamie has been kind enough to allow me to stay here until the divorce is finalized."

"I had in mind a few weeks, Auntie," said Jamie good-naturedly. "In actual fact, you've been here five months now."

"Don't exaggerate, dear. It's four and a bit."

"Are we the only guests?" said Hawk. "I can't believe we're the only Family come to pay our respects to the MacNeil."

"There are other guests," said Jamie. "They're upstairs in their rooms at present, but they'll be joining us for a late breakfast soon. We keep very relaxed hours here, especially since the servants left. But it must be said there aren't nearly as many Family here as one might have wished for."

"Why not?" asked Fisher bluntly.

The three MacNeils exchanged a quick glance. "I take it you've never heard of the MacNeil Curse," said Jamie slowly. "Not really surprising, I suppose, buried as you are in the depths of Lower Markham. It's not something we're proud of, and we don't care to discuss it with outsiders. But since you are both Family, and you've come all this way to be here . . . The Curse is the reason why so few have come to pay their respects, even with the reading of the will to tempt them. It's why the servants ran away, and why the Quality no longer accept invitations to Tower MacNeil. Please, be seated, all of you, and I'll tell you of the secret Shame of the MacNeils, and how it has come back to haunt us. I think it's time for the truth."

Everyone found themselves chairs, and drew them up in a semicircle facing the fireplace. Jamie stayed where he was, with his back to the fire, standing almost to attention, with his hands clasped behind his back, so the others wouldn't see them shaking. When he finally spoke, his voice was low and even and very controlled.

"Most people have heard something about the Curse of the MacNeils. That there is a monster which haunts us, and has done for generations. There have been many songs about it, and even one or two plays. Romantic fictions, all of them. We don't object; they help conceal the reality behind the myth. There is a Secret in our Family, handed down from father to eldest son alone, from generation to generation.

"Long ago, in the days before proper records were kept, a child was born to the MacNeils, to the head of the Family at that time. That child was the eldest son, destined to continue the Family bloodline. Unfortunately, he was also horribly deformed. He should have been killed at birth, but the MacNeil was a kind and tender-hearted man. The creature was, after all, his son. Perhaps a cure could be found. The MacNeil all but bankrupted the Family trying to find it, paying for doctors and sorcerers and healers of all kinds, but no cure was ever found.

"The creature became increasingly violent, and eventually had to be put away, for everyone's safety. The MacNeil took full responsibility for his awful son, and none of the Family or servants ever saw it again. Finally, some years later, the creature died, and everyone heaved a sigh of relief. The normal second son became the eldest son, the bloodline continued through him, and everything returned to normal.

"That is not the Secret. The songs and the romances and the plays are based loosely on what I have just told you, and from those distorted stories come the vague rumours that most people mean when they refer to the Curse of the MacNeils. The Secret, handed down from father to eldest son, is very simple. The creature did not die.

"The MacNeil had finally despaired of his monstrous son, and decided it should die, to free the Family of its burden. He gave the creature poison to drink, and walled up its room. He and the second son did the job themselves, rather than risk bringing in workmen or servants who might have talked. And all the time they laboured with bricks and mortar, they could hear the creature pacing restlessly back and forth in its cell. The poison did not kill it. Time and again the MacNeil and his son returned to listen at the wall they'd built, but though the creature had no access to food or water, still it lived. They could hear it moving about in its cell, and sometimes scratching at the walls.

"Years passed. The MacNeil died, and later so did his son, but the creature lived on. No one ever knew of its existence save the head of the Family and the eldest son, the Secret passing from generation to generation when the son reached his majority. And so it went, down all the many years.

"Only this time, something went wrong. My father

passed on the Secret to his eldest son, my brother William. But William died just three weeks ago, in a riding accident, and then my father was killed in a border clash, before he could pass on the details of the Secret to me. I was able to piece together what I've just told you from studying his papers after his death, but that's as far as his notes go. Presumably there are other papers somewhere, prepared in case of an emergency, but I've been unable to find them. No doubt Dad would have got around to telling me where they were, just in case . . . but who would ever have thought he'd die so suddenly. . . .''

Jamie stopped abruptly as his voice broke. Holly rose quickly from her seat and moved forward to hug her brother's arm protectively.

''Is that why the servants left?'' said Hawk. ''Because the Secret got out?''

Jamie shook his head. ''Not long after Dad died, the servants began seeing things. A dark figure, padding through the corridors late at night, or in the early hours of the morning. It always disappeared when challenged. I had the Tower searched from top to bottom by my security people, but they never found anyone. Then, things started to be broken. Vases, glasses, crockery. A chair was found smashed to pieces. Noises were heard at night; something that might have been screams, or laughter. My people began to leave, despite all I could offer them in the way of money or reassurances.

''Even my security people wouldn't stay. They all thought it was the ghost of my father, come back to haunt the Tower. Only I knew better. After all these years, the creature had finally got out. Obviously some part of the Secret dealt with how to keep it confined, and since I didn't know what to do . . . So far, it hasn't been able to leave Tower MacNeil; the Tower's protective wards see to that.''

''Why haven't you called in the city Guard?'' asked Fisher. ''Maybe their experts could find the creature. . . .''

''No!'' said Jamie sharply. ''This is Family business, and it has to stay within the Family. If the Secret ever gets out, the whole world will know the MacNeil Family is based on a lie. That all of us are descended from a *second* son. The Quality would declare that we had betrayed our bloodline and inheritance, and the MacNeils would be disgraced. Already there are rumours. That's why so few Family have come to declare their fealty to me.''

''Apart from us, who else knows the Secret?'' said Hawk.

''Just Greaves, my immediate Family, and my other guests, so far.''

''This . . . creature,'' said Fisher slowly. ''Has it tried to hurt anyone?''

''Not so far,'' said Jamie. ''But it is getting more destructive. Why? Do you want to leave?''

Hawk smiled slightly. ''I don't think so. Isobel and I don't scare easily.''

Katrina stirred in her chair. ''I can't believe Duncan kept the Secret so long. I had no idea . . . You're quite right, of course, Jamie. The Secret must never get out. We would be ostracised in High Society. Now then, the creature undoubtedly hides by day in the room that used to be its cell. Are you still unable to locate it?''

''I'm afraid so.'' Jamie's brow furrowed, and he ran a hand through his hair. ''The Tower is riddled with secret passages and sliding panels. I know some of them, and Dad's papers revealed a few more, but I still haven't been able to find where the creature is hiding. Presumably the room's location was part of the Secret.''

''This is crazy,'' said Fisher. ''If this creature was walled up for centuries, what kept it alive? Everything feeds on something. . . .''

''I don't know,'' said Jamie. ''But whatever the creature is, it's definitely not human. Maybe it hasn't died because it can't . . .''

For a long moment, nobody said anything. The crackling of the fire seemed very loud on the quiet.

''All this started because your father died unexpectedly,'' said Hawk finally. ''Just how did he die?''

Katrina looked at him sharply. ''You don't know?''

''Word often gets garbled when it has to travel long distances,'' said Fisher smoothly. "We want to make sure we've got it right.''

"I was just wondering,'' said Hawk carefully, "If perhaps there had been something unusual about your father's death . . . something that might give us a clue as to how the creature got out of its cell, after centuries of confinement. I mean, its room was supposed to have been bricked up. So how did it finally get out?''

"I see.'' Jamie nodded respectfully. "I hadn't thought of that. But no, there was nothing suspicious about my father's death. He was killed in a skirmish with Outremer troops up in the Northern borderlands. He shouldn't really have been there, an officer of his rank. But there had been rumours of new troop movements, and he wanted to see for himself. Dad was like that. Never really trusted anyone's opinion but his own. Anyway, he was in the wrong place at the wrong time, and he and his whole column were wiped out. Just another borderland skirmish. There's been a number of them just recently. Men are dying up there every day, just because our King and the Outremer Monarch can't agree on exactly where the bloody border is. Good men dying for a line on a map . . . I'm sorry. But it's hard not to be bitter sometimes. Dad was a good soldier. He deserved a better end than this. But I don't see how it could have had anything to do with the creature's escape.''

"Did anything . . . unusual happen here at the Tower, before the servants started seeing and hearing things?'' said Fisher.

Jamie thought for a moment. "I don't think so. I remember we were a bit short-staffed for a while about then. A lot of the servants had been going down with colds, but you expect that at this time of the year. A day off, and they were back at work again.''

"There's really nothing to worry about,'' said Katrina firmly. "You'll be quite safe here, I assure you. There's no indication the creature's ever tried to hurt anyone. That is right, isn't it, Jamie?''

"Yes, it is. But I felt it only fair you should all know what the situation is. You see, before the will can be read, the Tower has to be isolated behind protective wards for twenty-four hours. That's traditional.''

"You mean, once the wards are up, no one can leave the Tower for a full day?'' said Hawk. "No matter what happens here?''

He and Fisher exchanged a quick glance.

"That's right,'' said Jamie. "But trust me, nothing's going to happen. If the creature had meant any harm, it would have acted by now. All those years of imprisonment must have knocked the fight out of it.''

"I'm sure you're right,'' said Fisher. "But you couldn't have known that, at the beginning. In fact, it must have been pretty scary, especially when the servants started leaving, rather than face whatever it was. So why did you stay? Wouldn't it have been safer to evacuate the Tower?''

"This is my home,'' said Jamie. "Home to my Family for generations. I won't be driven out of it.''

There was an uncomfortable pause.

"Well,'' said Katrina brightly, "if all else fails, we can always call on the Guardian!''

"Who?'' said Hawk.

There was another, longer pause as the MacNeils looked at him strangely. Hawk silently cursed. He knew he should have insisted on a full briefing. Nothing was more likely to trip him and Fisher up than not recognizing some Family in-joke or reference, and this was clearly one of them. Still, the harm was done now. All he could do was try and face it down. He stared innocently back at Jamie and Katrina, and noticed for the first time that Holly wasn't paying any attention to the conversation. Instead, her eyes were far away, as though she were lost in some world of her own. Then Katrina started speaking, and Hawk quickly switched his attention back to her.

"You must have heard of the MacNeil Guardian,'' said Katrina, speaking slowly and carefully, as though to a rather backward small child. "Perhaps you know him by a different name. The Guardian is one of our more pleasant and comforting Family legends. One of our more remote ancestors is supposed to haunt the Tower, duty bound to protect his descendants from harm. Apparently it's a penance for some bloody crime he later came to regret but was unable to put right while he lived. The legend doesn't say exactly what his crime might have been.''

"That's often the way with legends," said Hawk. "You're right, of course. I recognize it now. Has anyone seen this ghost in recent times?"

"No one's seen him for centuries," said Jamie. "Though there have been any number of times when the Family could have used his help. So I'm afraid it is just a legend, after all.''

"I believe in him," said Holly suddenly. "I pray every night he'll come to save me. But he never does."

Everyone looked at her strangely for a moment. For the first time, there had been real passion in her voice, and something that might have been despair. Jamie looked at her worriedly, but said nothing, and Holly quickly subsided into silence again. Katrina cleared her throat loudly.

"That's supposed to be a portrait of the Guardian," she said brightly, indicating a dark and gloomy portrait directly over the fireplace. "Painted not long before his death. It's certainly old enough, so who knows?"

They all looked at the portrait. The pigments had darkened gradually over the years, but the image was still clear. The portrait showed a grim, unsmiling middle-aged man, posed uncomfortably in a large upholstered chair. He was dressed in battered leather armour, and his face was lined and weathered. He looked as though he would have been more at home riding a horse into combat than sitting for an official Family portrait. There was an air of strength and wildness about him, and his great mane of white hair and sharp, beaked nose reminded Hawk uncannily of a bird of prey, trained to duty but never tamed. Hawk had no trouble at all seeing him as a man who would do bloody crimes in the heat of passion.

Everyone jumped slightly as the door behind them swung suddenly open and the butler Greaves entered. He stepped to one side, and formally announced the arrival of Marc and Alistair MacNeil. The two men entered together, though with enough space between them to suggest they were neither comfortable nor happy in each other's company. They both bowed briefly to Jamie MacNeil.

Marc was tall and slender, with a broad, bland face and a cool, unhappy smile. He looked to be in his late twenties, if you ignored his prematurely thinning hair, and he wore the latest fashion poorly, as though indifferent to the effect it was supposed to achieve. He looked like the kind of man who attaches himself to groups at parties, in the hope someone will talk to him. His handshake was harsh and perfunctory, and his lips lingered almost obnoxiously over Fisher's hand. Jamie introduced him as another distant cousin, from Upper Markham.

"That makes him almost a neighbour of yours," said Jamie, smiling happily at Hawk and Fisher. "I'm sure you'll have lots in common to talk about."

"Oh good," said Hawk.

Marc sniffed. "I rather doubt it. No one worth knowing ever came out of *Lower* Markham."

There was an icy silence. Hawk's hand fell to his belt, before remembering he didn't have his axe any more. Fisher quickly dropped a restraining hand on his arm. Marc smiled stiffly, almost as though daring Hawk to take offense at such an obvious truth.

"That's enough!" said Jamie sharply. "There will be no duels in the Tower while I'm the MacNeil. Now apologize, Marc."

"Of course," said Marc. "I'm sorry."

His tone made the apology sound like another insult. Hawk's scowl deepened. Fisher tightened her grip on his arm. Hawk bowed stiffly, and turned his back on Marc to greet Alistair MacNeil. Marc sniffed again, and turned away to help himself to a drink from one of the wine decanters set out on the sideboard. Fisher breathed a silent sigh of relief, let go of Hawk's arm, and took a long drink from her glass.

Alistair shook Hawk's hand firmly, and kissed Fisher's hand with old-fashioned style. He smiled at them both, an open, friendly smile that did much to dispel the cool atmosphere left by Marc's comments. "Good of you to make such a long journey; it can't have been easy, getting here from Lower Markham at this time of the year."

"We felt we ought to be here," said Fisher. "Did you have far to come?"

"Quite a way. I'm another of those cousins the Family doesn't like to admit to knowing. I was brought up here in the Tower, but the Family packed me off to the Red Marches when I was a young man. Got a parlour maid into trouble and couldn't pay my gambling debts. Nothing too outrageous, but someone thought I needed to be made an example of, so off I went. Can't say I regret it. I could have come back long ago, but never saw the point. Lovely area, the Red Marches. Marvelous scenery, good hunting, and always a chance for some action on the borders. That's how I heard about Duncan's death. Beastly bad luck, by all accounts. So, I decided it was time to come back and pay my respects to the new MacNeil. Good of you to put me up, Jamie. I couldn't stick Haven. Place has gone to the dogs. Not at all how I remember it."

Hawk studied the man unobtrusively while he spoke. Alistair MacNeil was tall and muscular, though obviously well into his fifties. His stomach was intimidatingly flat, his back poker straight, and if Alistair was carrying a few extra pounds anywhere, Hawk was damned if he could spot them. His clothes were undeniably old-fashioned but exquisitely cut, and Alistair wore them with unconscious style. His iron-grey hair was cropped close to his head, military fashion, but he had the same beaked nose and piercing eyes as the man in the portrait. Alistair caught Hawk glancing from him to the portrait over the fire, and chuckled dryly.

"There is a resemblance, isn't there? You're not the first to spot it. Doesn't look such a bad type to me. Probably just too much energy and not enough wars to keep him occupied."

"Don't glorify the man," said Marc, staring up at the portrait, a large drink in his hand. "A soldier in those days was just a paid killer, nothing more. All his masters had to do was point him in the right direction and turn him loose.

Probably killed women and children too if they got in his way.''

''They were hard times,'' said Alistair coldly. ''The Low Kingdoms faced threats on all sides. The minstrels like to sing of honour and glory, but there's damn all glory for the quick or the dead on a battlefield. There's just the blood and the flies, and the knowledge it will all have to be done again tomorrow. You should try a spell in the army yourself, Marc. You might learn a few things.''

''If you say so,'' said Marc. He turned his back on Alistair, and stared coldly at Jamie. ''May I enquire how much longer we have to wait before the reading of the will? The sooner this tedious ritual is over and done with, the better. The Tower is undoubtedly charming, for its age, but I have business to attend to in Haven.''

''We'll get to the will soon enough,'' said Jamie evenly. ''There are two more guests to join us, and then breakfast will be served. I think we'll all feel better for a good meal before getting down to business.''

''I'm not hungry,'' said Marc.

''You speak for yourself,'' said Hawk.

The door opened, and a faded-looking jester hurried in, unannounced by the butler. At least Hawk assumed the man was a jester. He couldn't see any other reason for wearing an outfit like that, short of an extremely convincing death threat. Personally speaking, Hawk would rather have taken his chances with the death threat. The newcomer was a rotund little man, brimming with eager nervous energy. His bright eyes flashed indiscriminately in every direction, much like his smile, and his quick bow to Jamie MacNeil was little more than a familiar nod. The newcomer was well into his sixties, and looked it, but his costume looked to be even older. It had clearly started out life as a bright and gaudy coat of many colors, but over the many years the colors had faded, stitches had burst, and a whole mess of new patches, clearly more functional than decorative, had been added. And then, finally, Hawk saw the guitar in the man's hand, and his heart sank. Jamie smiled briefly at the man, and then turned to his guests.

"My friends, this is my minstrel, Robbie Brennan. Been with this Family for almost thirty years, haven't you, Robbie? I have to leave for a moment, so play something for my guests; some tale of my father's exploits, in his memory."

Brennan nodded cheerfully, tried a few quick dissonant chords, and launched into an uptempo ballad. He sang three songs altogether, each of them highly romanticized tales of Duncan MacNeil's past. They were all cut from the same cloth, full of great adventures and daring escapes, but though they couldn't seem to decide whether Duncan had been a saint or a warrior, a mighty lover or a devoted family man, they all had one thing in common: All three songs were irredeemably awful. They were badly written, played with no style and too much feeling, and Brennan's voice was all over the place. He had the kind of singing voice that made you long for the sound of fingernails scraping down a blackboard, and an extremely irritating habit of shifting his voice up or down an octave when he couldn't reach the right note.

Hawk's hands closed into fists halfway through the first song. By the second, Fisher had to physically restrain him by clinging determinedly but unobtrusively to his arm. Hawk didn't care much for minstrels at the best of times, which this definitely wasn't, and he had a particular loathing for this kind of smug, cleaned-up hero worship. He usually tended to express this unhappiness by throwing the offending minstrel through the nearest window. Fisher, feeling strongly that this might not go down too well with Jamie MacNeil, clung firmly to Hawk's sword arm with both hands.

Brennan finally ground to a halt in a series of crashing chords and bowed more or less gracefully to his stunned audience. There was scattered applause, possibly out of relief that the performance was over. Hawk was grinding his teeth behind a fixed smile.

"Clap him, dammit," said Fisher, out of the corner of her mouth.

"Forget it," growled Hawk. "If we encourage him, he might do an encore. And I swear if I hear one more heynonny-no out of him, I'm going to ram his fingers up his nose till they stick out his ears.''

Katrina got the minstrel a drink, and the two of them stood chatting together. Jamie came back into the room and went over to join Hawk and Fisher. He checked to make sure Brennan wasn't watching, and then shook his head ruefully.

''He's not very good, is he? Sorry to put you through that, but it's expected of me that I have my own minstrel. Family tradition and all that. Robbie was my father's minstrel, and I seem to have inherited him. He hasn't improved over the years. Dad had cloth ears, but liked to sing, even though he couldn't carry a tune in a bucket. Robbie suited him very well. Besides, when all is said and done, he and Dad fought back to back on a dozen major campaigns, when they were both a lot younger. Least I can do is give Robbie a safe berth at the end of his days. I just wish I could convince him to retire. . . .''

He looked round as the door opened yet again, and the butler Greaves ushered in two more guests. Hawk looked too, and his stomach lurched as though one of his feet had just slipped over the edge of a precipice. He knew one of the men in the doorway, and worse still, that man knew Captain Hawk. Jamie moved quickly over to greet the new arrivals, grinning broadly. Hawk struck his best aristocratic pose, and smiled determinedly. It seemed he was about to find out just how good his disguise really was.

Lord Arthur Sinclair smiled graciously at Jamie and strolled amiably forward into the drawing room, wineglass in hand, blinking vaguely about him. He was short, barely five foot tall, and sufficiently overweight so that he looked even shorter. He had a round, guileless face and smiled a lot at nothing in particular, but his uncertain blue eyes gave him a lost, confused look. He was in his mid-thirties, with thinning yellow hair and the beginnings of a truly impressive set of jowls. He was also a drunk.

He had no talents and no abilities, and thanks to his Family, little or no self-esteem. He spent most of his time at parties, while the more conservative members of High

Society murmured darkly that he'd no doubt come to a bad end. To the surprise of everyone, not least himself, he'd inherited all his Family's wealth, and for want of anything better to do had spent the last few years trying to drink himself to death. All in all, he was making a pretty good job of it; the first and only time he'd made a success of anything. He dabbled occasionally in politics, just for the fun of it, and had briefly been a member of the infamous Hellfire Club. Which was where Hawk had met him, while working on a case. Hawk tried not to feel too worried. Sinclair had been pretty drunk when they met. But then, he usually was. . . .

Fisher, meanwhile, had been keeping an eye on the other new arrival. Jamie had introduced him to the room at large as David Brook, an old friend. Like most people in Haven, Fisher had heard of the Brook Family; they had a long tradition of high achievement in the army and the diplomatic corps. To excel in one or the other was not unusual, but to excel in both was almost unheard of. Particularly in Haven, where diplomacy was usually just another way of sneaking up on an enemy when he wasn't looking. But, that was the Brooks for you; brave and intelligent. A deadly combination.

David himself was a brisk, heavyset man of slightly less than average height, well into his late twenties, and dressed impeccably if somewhat gaudily in the very latest fashion. He clapped Jamie companionably on the shoulder, and strode forward to shake hands with the bemused Hawk. He lingered acceptably over Fisher's hand as he kissed it, and Fisher's smile widened approvingly, almost in spite of herself. David Brook was devilishly handsome, in a dark, swarthy way. And he knew it.

He excused himself with polished regret, and moved quickly over to join Holly. She smiled shakily at him with open relief, and for the first time that morning, some of the fear seemed to go out of her. She and David smiled and murmured together with the ease of long affection, their heads so close as to be almost touching. Lord Sinclair shook Hawk's hand and kissed Fisher's, smiling vaguely all the while, and then wandered over to join David and Holly, blinking owlishly as he waited to be noticed. They broke apart reluctantly, and Holly smiled at Sinclair with the kind of resigned affection usually reserved for puppies that are cute and lovable but only barely housebroken.

Jamie returned to top up Hawk's glass, and he nodded gratefully. Jamie noticed Hawk's interest in Holly's admirers, and he raised an eyebrow. "Do you know David or Arthur?"

"No," said Hawk quickly. "But I have heard of Lord Arthur. I understand he likes his drink. . . ."

Jamie snorted. "That's like saying a fish likes swimming. But you don't want to believe everything you hear. Arthur's a decent enough sort, when you get to know him. He and David have always been close. And Holly and David have been practically engaged since they were ten. Childhood sweethearts, and all that. And I'll say this for Arthur; he stuck by us when all our other so-called friends ran for cover."

"He wouldn't be the first to find courage in a bottle," said Marc, appearing as usual seemingly out of nowhere. "Probably too drunk and too foolish to be scared."

"You think so?" said Jamie. His voice was polite, but his eyes were hard.

Marc sniffed. "I know his sort."

"No," said Jamie. "You don't know him at all. Now, if you'll excuse me, I have to consult with Greaves about breakfast."

He smiled at Hawk and Fisher, nodded briefly to Marc, and left. Hawk didn't blame him. Marc's voice had the kind of insensitive arrogance that would have had a saint's hands curling into fists. Fisher fixed Marc with a thoughtful stare.

"You don't approve of Lord Arthur?"

"He's weak. I despise weakness. You have to be strong in this world or it'll grind you under."

"We can't all be strong," said Fisher.

Marc smiled coldly. "You don't have to be. You're beautiful. There will always be someone ready to be strong for you."

He turned away, ignoring Hawk's glare, and went to stare out the wide window at the morning sunlight.

"Take it easy," said Fisher amusedly to Hawk. "We're supposed to be brother and sister, remember?"

"So I'm a very protective brother. Watch yourself with that one, Isobel. I don't trust him."

"I don't trust any of them, but I take your point. Don't worry; I know how to handle his sort."

Hawk looked at her quickly. "We're Quality now; if there's to be any rough stuff, I'll take care of it. You concentrate on being demure and ladylike." Fisher raised an eyebrow, and Hawk had to smile. "Or at least as close as you can get."

Fisher gestured surreptitiously, and Hawk fell silent as Katrina Dorimant came over to join them. She nodded briefly to Fisher and then unleashed the full force of her smile on Hawk. It was a warm, intimate smile, suffused with promise, backed up by dark and unsettlingly direct eyes. Hawk smiled uncomfortably back, unconsciously standing a little taller and sucking in his gut. If Isobel hadn't been there he might have just relaxed and enjoyed it, but as it was . . . He glanced at Isobel and was relieved to find she was smiling, apparently amused at his discomfort. Hawk decided he'd better play this very carefully. On the one hand, he couldn't afford to antagonize his host's Aunt, but on the other hand, if Isobel stopped finding this funny long enough to get jealous . . . Hawk winced inwardly.

"I'm so glad you're here, Richard," said Katrina smoothly.

"Really?" said Hawk, his voice nowhere near as even as he would have liked.

"Oh yes," said Katrina. "I was starting to think I'd have to spend this weekend all alone. I do so hate to be alone."

"There are other guests here," Fisher pointed out.

Katrina shrugged, without taking her eyes off Hawk. "Alistair's too old, Arthur's too fat, David only has eyes for Holly, and Marc gives me the creeps. I don't like the way he looks at me. I'd begun to despair, until you arrived, Richard."

"I understand you're . . . separated from your husband," said Hawk, out of a feeling he ought to be contributing something to the conversation.

"That's right. My husband's Graham Dorimant, a sort of somebody in local politics. We're going to be divorced as soon as I can get the goods on him."

Hawk felt a strong inclination to turn and beat his head against the nearest wall. Was this case going to be nothing but one complication after another? Not only did he have to worry about Arthur Sinclair recognizing him, but now the woman who was making eyes at him turned out to be the estranged wife of someone else who knew him. Hawk and Fisher had met Graham Dorimant on a previous case, not all that long ago. If by some chance Graham had discussed that case with Katrina . . . A sudden thought sobered Hawk like a rush of cold water. Hawk and Fisher had made a great impression on Graham Dorimant. It could be that he'd described the two Guards he'd met fully enough for Katrina to recognize them even through their disguises. And if she had, what better way to distract them than by making a play for Hawk? But that assumed she had a reason for distracting them, which meant . . .

The door opened, and Greaves entered to announce that breakfast would be served shortly in the dining room. As everyone present moved towards the door, Katrina quickly latched onto Hawk's arm.

"It is good of you to escort me into breakfast, Richard. You will sit with me, won't you?"

"I ought really to sit with my sister," said Hawk, knowing how feeble it sounded even as he said it.

"Oh, don't mind me," said Fisher promptly. "You enjoy yourself, Richard."

Hawk gave her a hard look.

"Breakfast won't be much, I'm afraid," said Katrina chummily as they moved out into the corridor. "Cook left two days ago, along with what was left of the kitchen staff. But Greaves and Robbie Brennan have been managing between them until the new staff arrive."

Hawk looked at her sharply. "I thought you couldn't get servants to stay here, because of the sightings?"

Katrina laughed. "This is Haven, Richard. Money can buy anything here. They won't be top-notch staff, of course, but they'll do. Until we can sort this mess out. Now, what was I saying? Oh yes; breakfast. Cold collation, I'm afraid, but I suppose I shouldn't complain. It's very good for the figure, and I have been putting on a little weight recently."

She glanced coquettishly at Hawk, obviously expecting some chivalrous denial. He was still trying to come up with an answer that was both polite and noncommittal when they reached the dining room, at the end of the long, twisting corridor. The room was grand in design, if not in scale, most of it taken up by the single great table, which looked as though it could easily seat thirty, and another dozen or so if everyone was feeling chummy. A magnificent white tablecloth lay half hidden under the glistening silver service and three blazing candelabra.

Everyone took seats at one end of the table with a minimum of fuss, and Hawk ended up with Katrina on one side and Fisher on the other. Arthur Sinclair was sitting opposite him, and Hawk's heart missed a beat as that gentleman suddenly leaned forward and addressed him.

"Tell me . . . Richard?"

"Yes."

"Yes, Richard . . . something I've been meaning to ask you. Why is your hair black and your sister's yellow?"

"Mother was frightened by an albatross," said Hawk solemnly.

Lord Arthur blinked at him, nodded, and returned his attention to his wineglass. Hawk looked at the setting in front of him and panicked briefly as he found he didn't even recognize some of the more sophisticated cutlery. *Start at the outside and work inwards*, he told himself firmly, reaching for the outer knife and fork. *It's got prongs on it; it's got to be a fork*. . . . Greaves and Robbie Brennan appeared through the swinging service door, carrying trays of cold meats and artfully arranged raw vegetables.

"When you're ready, Greaves, do you think you could

do something about the fire?'' said Jamie. ''It seems rather cold in here today.''

''Of course, sir.'' Greaves gestured for Brennan to put his trays down on the table and see to the fire. Brennan gave him a look, but did as he was bid.

For a while, there was only the occasional murmur of conversation as everyone heaped their plates and then set about the serious business of breakfast. Hawk in particular tucked into his food with gusto, but Marc, sitting opposite Fisher, seemed to be just toying with his. Hawk assumed he was one of those people who couldn't face a heavy meal first thing in the morning. Meanwhile, the minstrel had called on Greaves to help him get the fire going. Hawk smiled slightly. The butler obviously didn't care at all for being involved in such a menial task. He gave Brennan a hard look, and then reached gingerly up into the chimney to tug at some obstruction. Whatever it was, it didn't want to budge, and Greaves had to try again, harder. And then he and Brennan jumped back from the fireplace with cries of shock and horror as a body fell down out of the chimney and crashed into the grate. It was a man, entirely naked and stained with soot, and very obviously dead. The whole of his face had been burned away by the fire.

4

Wolf in the Fold

For a long moment nobody stirred, and then there was a general scramble round the table as people surged to their feet. Greaves backed away from the body, unable to take his eyes off it, until he bumped into the edge of the table behind him. Brennan stayed where he was, rooted to the spot. Hawk pushed past them both and knelt down beside the dead man. Jamie and Alistair crowded in behind him, peering over his shoulder but apparently unwilling to get any closer than that to the body. Fisher leaned gingerly into the fireplace and peered up the chimney, just in case it held any more nasty surprises. Everyone else huddled together at the far end of the table, torn between edging closer for a better look and making a mad dash for the door. Holly's face was bone white, and she clung desperately to Katrina for support. Katrina patted her niece's hands in an absent-minded, comforting way while she craned her neck to see what was happening. David and Arthur had both moved to put themselves between the ladies and the dead man, as much out of gallantry as anything. Marc stood beside them, gazing with fascination at the dead man.

Hawk did his best to ignore Jamie and Alistair breathing down his neck, and looked the dead man over carefully, starting at what was left of the head and working his way slowly down the body. There were a number of cuts and scrapes, presumably from being wedged up the chimney, but no sign of any death wound. He turned his attention back to the burned face, and winced despite himself. The eyes and nose were gone, and the teeth grinned horribly through a mask of charred flesh and bone. There was no hair left, and the ears were nothing more than blackened nubs. Hawk breathed shallowly through his mouth, trying to avoid the smell. He'd seen many dead men in his time, often in worse condition than this, but there was something disturbingly cold and calculating in the manner of this man's death. He touched the man's shoulder gently with his fingertips. The flesh was cold to the touch, already showing the purplish bruises caused by blood sinking to the lowest part of the body. The dead man had been in the chimney for some time. Maybe overnight. Hawk tried the neck, but it didn't seem to be broken. He worked the dead man's arm gently, and it bent easily at the elbow, indicating rigor mortis either hadn't set in yet or had been and gone. Hawk frowned. That was probably a clue as to how long the man had been dead, but he didn't understand such things. He'd never needed to. That was what forensic sorcerers were for. He looked round sharply as Jamie MacNeil crouched down beside him. Alistair leaned in closer, one hand resting supportively on Jamie's shoulder.

"How did he die, do you think?" said Jamie steadily.

"Hard to tell," said Hawk. "There's no actual death wound that I can see, just the damage to the face."

"Nasty way to go," said Alistair. "I once knew a tribe of savages who killed their prisoners this way; hung them over an open fire till their brains boiled. Nasty."

"I don't think that's what happened here," said Hawk slowly. "Look at the back of the head." He gingerly lifted the burned head off the floor so they could see. "The face has been totally destroyed, but the back of the head is barely touched. I think someone pushed this poor bastard's face into the fire and held it there till he died."

"Gods!" Jamie looked suddenly as though he might vomit, and turned his head away, eyes squeezed shut.

"There's no sign of any struggle here, as far as I can

see," said Fisher, her voice coming hollowly from inside the chimney. She ducked her head back out, and beat soot from her hair and shoulders. "Looks to me like he was already dead when the killer stuffed him up the chimney."

She started towards the group round the body, but Alistair moved quickly to block her way. "That's quite close enough, my dear. Please return to the others. This is no sight for a young lady such as yourself."

Fisher was about to ask sarcastically whether he was referring to the dead man's injuries or his nakedness, when she caught Hawk glaring at her. At which point she remembered she was supposed to be a sheltered young flower of the Quality, not a hardened city Guard, and she went reluctantly back to join the others. She put a comforting arm round Holly's shaking shoulders and listened carefully to what was being said about the dead man.

"Any idea who this is? Or rather, was?" said Hawk to Jamie.

The MacNeil looked back at the body. His face was very pale, but his gaze was steady and his mouth was firm. "Whoever he is, he shouldn't be here. The last of the servants left two days ago, and the only guests I know of are all in this room."

"Maybe one of the servants came back," said Alistair.

"Not without Greaves knowing, and he would have told me." Jamie shook his head slowly. "None of this makes any sense. No one could have got in past the Tower's wards without setting off all kinds of alarms. It's impossible. And besides; who would want to kill a man here, and like . . . that? It's insane!"

Alistair gripped Jamie's shoulder firmly. "Easy, lad. Don't go to pieces on us now. You're the MacNeil, and the others will be looking to you for guidance. We have a murderer loose in the Tower somewhere, and we have to find him. Before he strikes again."

"He's right," said Hawk. "This is a very nasty business, Jamie. You'd better call in the Guard."

"No!" said Alistair sharply. "This is a Family matter. We don't bring outsiders into Family business."

Hawk got to his feet and stared at Alistair. "What century are you living in ? You can't keep the Guard out of something like this! This is murder we're talking about, not who put some chambermaid up the stick. Our best bet is to get the hell out of here, send for the Guard, and then block off all the exits till they get here. Let them find the killer; they're experts."

"I'm afraid it's not that simple," said Jamie, rising to his feet. "I've already raised the final wards. I did it just now, so that we could get on with the reading of the will. I never thought . . . The wards can't be lowered for another twenty-four hours. That's the way they're designed. I'm sorry; there's nothing I can do. None of us can leave the Tower."

David Brook stepped forward, staring disbelievingly at Jamie. "Are you saying that we're all trapped in here with a killer? That whatever happens, there's no way out?"

"Yes," said Jamie. "I'm afraid so." He stopped abruptly and looked at Hawk, who was frowning down at the body. "What is it, Richard?"

"I was just wondering why the killer took the time to strip the body naked. Presumably the killer didn't want us to be able to identify the victim. Which suggests that at least one of us would have recognized him. That explains the burned face, as well."

There was a short pause, broken by Fisher. "Something else to think about. That body had been wedged quite a way up the chimney, going by the traces I found. Whoever the killer is, he must be pretty strong. It can't have been easy, stuffing a limp dead body feet first up a chimney."

Holly moaned quietly, and several of the others looked quite disturbed by Fisher's remark.

"The man must have been mad," said David. "Madmen are supposed to be incredibly strong, aren't they?"

Alistair cleared his throat meaningfully. "Thank you for sharing your thoughts with us, Isobel, but I really feel you and the other ladies should withdraw. This is not a subject suitable for your tender ears."

"No!" said Hawk quickly. "I don't want anyone going

off on their own. Unless they like the idea of being an easy target. Until we know what the hell's going on here, we'd do better to stick together. There's safety in numbers.''

Jamie looked at him strangely. ''You sound almost as though you've had experience with this sort of thing before, Richard.''

Being called Richard brought Hawk up short, as he remembered who he was supposed to be. He shrugged, thinking quickly. ''There was a murder at one of the inns Isobel and I stayed at on our way here. I did a lot of thinking about it afterwards, and all the sensible things I should have done. But you're the MacNeil, Jamie, and this is your home. You're in charge. I wasn't trying to usurp your authority.''

''Don't be daft,'' said Jamie. ''This is all new to me. If you've got any ideas on what we ought to be doing, speak out.''

''Well, to start with I think we should get back to the drawing room. I don't think we ought to move the body, and we can't hope to discuss this mess sensibly while it's lying right there in front of us.''

''Are you saying we should just leave the body here?'' said Robbie Brennan.

''Why not?'' said Alistair. ''It's not going anywhere.''

''At least cover him,'' said Katrina unsteadily. ''Give the poor man some dignity.''

''And just what are we supposed to cover him with?'' asked Marc. ''I'm afraid I didn't think to bring a shroud with me to breakfast.''

''Maybe someone could fetch a cloak from the main hall,'' said David.

''No!'' said Holly quickly. ''You heard Richard; it's not safe for anyone to go off on their own.''

''We can't just leave the man like this!'' said Katrina shrilly, with a stubbornness that bordered on hysteria. ''He's got to be covered decently!''

Fisher grabbed one end of the magnificent white tablecloth and gave it a good hard jerk. Food, china, cutlery, and flowers went flying in all directions. The candelabra collapsed, and rivers of spilled wine cascaded over the sides of the table as she kept pulling. The last of the tablecloth finally came free, and Fisher draped it roughly over the dead man. Jamie stared speechlessly at the mess she'd made, and then looked at her. She smiled back at him.

"Can we get the hell out of here now?" she said pointedly. "This place makes me nervous. Besides, I need a good stiff drink, and the good brandies are back in the drawing room."

Hawk fought to keep the smile off his lips. He should have known Fisher wouldn't be able to keep up the demure young lady pose for long. He supposed he should be grateful that at least she hadn't hit anyone yet. He coughed loudly to draw everyone's attention back to him.

"If we're going to move, let's move. If nothing else, I think we'll be safer in the drawing room. It's a lot easier to defend than this place. There are too many doors here for my liking."

Alistair nodded approvingly. "Good thinking, lad. The drawing room's only got one door, and we can barricade that if necessary."

Katrina's hand rose unsteadily to her mouth, and her eyes widened. "You mean the murderer might try and attack us?"

"It's possible," said Hawk. "We don't know what we're dealing with yet."

"I think you're all worrying needlessly," said Marc. "This is one man we're talking about, not an army. If worst comes to worst, there are more than enough of us here to overpower him."

"It might not be that simple," said Jamie slowly. "There's only one man who could have done something like this. The freak. He's got out, after all these years, and he wants revenge. Revenge on the Family that walled him up alive."

Silence fell across the dining room as they all looked at each other, the tension almost crackling on the air. Hawk silently cursed the young MacNeil. He'd already worked out that the freak was most likely the murderer, but he'd wanted the others safely back in the drawing room before he told them. The last thing he needed was a panic here. He tried his cough again, and everyone's eyes shot to him.

"There'll be time to discuss all this later," he said firmly. "Right now, I want everyone concentrating on getting back to the drawing room safely."

"What gives you the right to give everyone orders?" said Marc. "Why should we listen to you?"

"Because he's talking sense," said Jamie. "All right, Richard, let's take a look out in the corridor and make sure it's clear."

The two of them moved over to the main door, eased it open a crack, then took turns peering out down the corridor. Nothing moved in the clear morning light, and the few shadows were comfortingly small. Jamie looked at Hawk.

"How do you want to do this, Richard?"

Hawk frowned. "First thing, all the men draw their swords. Just in case. I'll go first, then you and Alistair. The women will come after us, with the rest of the men bringing up the rear." He looked back at the others and gave them his best reassuring smile. "There's no reason for anyone to be worried. We're just taking sensible precautions, that's all."

None of them looked particularly convinced. Hawk sighed, and gave up on the smile. He'd always done better with a glare than a smile. He looked at Jamie for help, and the MacNeil quickly got everyone moving with a brisk mixture of tact and authority. Hawk nodded approvingly. Jamie had the right touch; that particular mixture of arrogance and charm that was the hallmark of the aristocracy. Hawk led them out into the corridor, and headed back to the drawing room at a carefully unhurried pace. It wouldn't do to take it too quickly; most of them were so rattled they'd break into a run first chance they got. And that would be a real recipe for disaster. Once they were all just running wildly, the freak could pick any one of them off without being noticed. So Hawk strode along at a casual pace, carefully checking each turn of the corridor as he came to it. Luckily he had a good head for direction. Unlike Isobel. She could get lost going to the jakes in a strange inn, and had done, before now.

The corridor seemed subtly different than it had the last time he'd walked it. The light grew dimmer as they left the windows behind them, and came to depend more and more on the wall lamps. The shadows grew darker and larger, and it was easy to imagine something cruel and menacing waiting patiently in the darkness for them to pass. Every door was a potential threat, every turn in the corridor a potential trap. The quiet seemed increasingly sinister, broken only by the soft scuffing and shuffling of their feet on the polished floor. Hawk hefted the light duelling sword in his hand, and wished more than ever for his axe.

He scowled furiously as he tried to figure out what to do next. The last time he and Fisher had been trapped in an isolated house with a group of guests and a killer on the loose, things had gone terribly wrong. He and Fisher had put a stop to the killings eventually, but not before too many innocent people had died. Hawk's frown deepened. He was damned if he'd let that happen again. He tensed and lifted his sword as someone came up alongside him, but it was only Alistair.

"Hold your water, lad, it's just me. Wanted to congratulate you on how you're handling things. You've had military experience, haven't you?"

"Actually no," said Hawk. "I know it's not really my place to be taking charge and giving orders, but everyone else seemed too shaken, and there were things that needed to be done. We weren't safe in the dining room."

"You'll get no arguments from me on that, lad. I haven't felt easy in the Tower since I arrived. Place feels . . . secretive. But . . . do you really think the freak is that dangerous? He's only one man."

Hawk scowled unhappily. "I don't know. He's a mystery, and I don't like mysteries. When you get right down to it, the freak is most dangerous because he doesn't fit any normal pattern. Most murders involve people who know each other, people who kill either for business reasons or in the heat of passion. But we're dealing with someone who's spent centuries in solitary confinement, building his madness year by year and honing his hate to a cutting edge. He could do anything, for any reason; which means we haven't a hope in hell of out-thinking him. All we can do is stack the odds in our favour as much as we can.''

''Very sensible,'' said Alistair. He looked thoughtfully at Hawk. ''No offence, Richard, but you do seem to know an uncommon lot about murders and murderers. Mind telling me how you came by that knowledge?''

''Of course not,'' said Hawk, thinking quickly. ''There's not much to do in Lower Markham, so I read a lot. Crime fascinates me. Especially murders. So that's what I read about. Mostly.''

Alistair made no comment, just nodded and dropped back to rejoin Jamie. Hawk sighed. It wasn't the best answer he could have come up with, but then, thinking on his feet had never been what he did best. Except when he was fighting. But he was going to have to be more careful. He had to think like a Guard if he was going to solve this case, but he couldn't afford to act like one. If Jamie was to find out he'd revealed his Family's darkest Secret to an outsider, and a city Guard at that . . .

There was a collective sigh of relief as they hurried down the last stretch of corridor and reached the drawing room without incident. Hawk was first in, and quickly checked the room was secure. He then ushered the others in, and checked the door for bolts. There weren't any, so he wedged a chair up against the door and settled for that. Some of the tension went out of him, and he let out a long, weary sigh. In a situation like this, looking out for yourself was tiring enough, without having to worry about a bunch of civilians, half of whom were jumping at their own damn shadows.

They were already splitting up into smaller groups, turning to those they trusted most for comfort and support. Jamie and Alistair were talking urgently together, with a fair amount of arm waving from both of them. David Brook and Lord Arthur were trying to help Katrina soothe Holly, who was still trembling pitifully. Marc stood with them, holding a drink for Holly, his face as calm and composed as ever.

Hawk studied him a moment, frowning thoughtfully. Of them all, Marc had coped best with the situation. He might well prove a useful ally if things started getting out of control. Whatever else you could say about Marc, the man had guts. Hawk looked away, and his gaze settled on Brennan and Greaves. They were standing patiently together not far from Jamie and Alistair, waiting for orders. Fisher came over to join Hawk with a snifter of brandy in each hand. Hawk accepted his gratefully.

"Well?" said Fisher. "How do you read this? What the hell's going on here?"

Hawk shrugged. "You got me. What little evidence there is points in half a dozen different directions at once. I did some thinking on the way here, and I've managed to narrow it down to three main possibilities. First, and most obvious, is that the freak really has got loose, and has graduated from breaking up the furniture to killing people. That doesn't explain who the dead stranger is, though, or why the freak chose him as his first victim, rather than one of us.

"Second choice, equally obvious: This is all something to do with the spy Fenris. Perhaps the dead man was to be Fenris' contact, and someone killed him to prevent that contact taking place. Or, the dead man could be Fenris, killed by his contact for screwing up his mission. That would explain why the man's face was burned away, so that we wouldn't be able to tell who Fenris really was.

"And finally, there's choice number three: Someone in this room is a murderer, and killed that man for personal reasons that have nothing to do with Fenris or the freak."

"Great," said Fisher. "Just what we needed. As if this case wasn't complicated enough, we now have a murder mystery on our hands. Great. Bloody marvelous. All right, what do we do? Reveal who we are and take charge?"

"Are you crazy?" said Hawk. "The penalty for impersonating Quality is death by dismemberment, remember? Besides, we don't dare risk our cover until we've got some kind of lead on which of these people is Fenris. Our orders were to prevent Fenris escaping, *no matter what*. We're going to have to do what sleuthing we can undercover, and keep our ideas to ourselves.''

"That shouldn't be too difficult," said Fisher. "I haven't got two ideas to rub together."

"Then you haven't been paying attention. We already know Alistair isn't being honest about where he comes from.''

"We do?" Fisher looked at him sternly. "You're showing off again, *Richard*. All right, what did I miss this time?''

Hawk couldn't keep all the smile off his lips. "According to Alistair, he comes from the Red Marches. He grew almost lyrical about the marvelous countryside, and the good hunting to be found there. But we passed through the Red Marches on our way to Haven, seven years ago. They've been flooded for the past eighty years. Most of the land is under water now. There's some good fishing here and there, but no hunting. He also talked about getting involved in fighting down on the border, but thanks to the floods, it's been peaceful down there for years. It's the most secure border in the Low Kingdoms these days. But Alistair didn't know that. Interesting, eh?''

"Very," said Fisher. "But why didn't any of the others pick up on it?''

Hawk shrugged. "The Red Marches are pretty remote, and about as far from High Society as you can get. It's probably just a name to most people here. Which is probably what Alistair was counting on.''

"I'll tell you who else we ought to keep an eye on," said Fisher, "And that's Katrina. She's still married to Graham Dorimant, who was heavily involved in the local political scene. Since they're separated now, and not at all amicably, it's just possible she might have got involved in outsider politics as a way of getting back at her husband. She could be Fenris' contact. She's been here at the Tower for some time; that could explain why Fenris went to ground here.''

"But if he's already met his contact, why hasn't he left?''

"Perhaps he's waiting for her to arrange a safe route out.''

"Hold your horses," said Hawk suddenly. "There's another possibility, and one we should have spotted sooner. What if the dead man had been Fenris' contact, and had threatened to abandon Fenris to the authorities, rather than risk any more of the outsider network being discovered? Fenris must know he's facing a death penalty, even if he is Quality. He could have killed his contact to protect himself, and then hidden the body while he tried to figure out what to do next.''

''Right,'' said Fisher. ''But he left it too late, and Jamie put the wards up. We've got to identify him before tomorrow, Hawk, or he'll do a runner the moment the wards go down.''

''Isobel, will you please call me Richard! Walls have ears, you know, especially in a situation like this.''

''Sorry. But if Fenris is our killer, it means we can stop wasting time looking for some imaginary murderous freak. I mean, what proof have we the creature ever existed, apart from Jamie's story?''

Hawk shrugged. ''We've seen stranger things in our time.''

On the other side of the room, Jamie looked at Alistair almost pleadingly. ''We can talk about Richard and Isobel later, Alistair. I've more important things to worry about. What am I going to do about the killing? I'm the MacNeil, the head of the Family; they'll all be looking to me for reassurance and answers I haven't got, and I don't know what to do!''

''To start with, calm down,'' said Alistair sharply. ''Getting hysterical won't help. Let's look at this logically. Now that we know the freak's a killer, what matters most is tracking it down before it strikes again. Which means we have to find the hidden cell. We'll search the Tower from top to bottom, checking each room as we go for hidden panels and secret passages. If the freak got out of his room, there must be a way in. We can split into two groups to save time. I'll take one group, you lead the other. Right?''

''Yes. Right.'' Jamie breathed deeply twice, and pinched the bridge of his nose hard. It seemed to help. The panic that had all but paralysed him was dropping swiftly away, now that he had a definite goal to focus on. He smiled quickly at Alistair and looked around him. "There's no point in taking everyone with us. The women will be safer here, out of harm's way."

"We'd better leave Lord Arthur behind as well." Alistair's voice was mild, but his gaze was unyielding. "I think he means well, but you can't trust a drunk in a crisis. What about David Brook? Good man?"

"The best," said Jamie. "Good with a sword, level-headed, and doesn't scare easily. Always knows the right thing to do in a tricky situation. I'd trust him with my life. We'll take Greaves, too. He's another steady one; utterly dependable. As for Robbie Brennan . . . he's a stout enough man, and damned good with a sword in his younger days, from what Dad used to say. But that was a long time ago."

"Once a soldier, always a soldier," said Alistair. "The old instincts will still be there, just needing the right moment to bring them out again."

"If you say so. What about Marc?"

Alistair frowned. "He's a cool one, I'll give him that, but I don't know if I'd trust him to guard my back. Still, he doesn't look the type to fold under pressure. And that just leaves Richard. And you know how I feel about him. . . ."

"He seems a solid enough sort," said Jamie. "Somewhat gauche and a bit of a bumpkin, but this is his first trip to the big city, after all. And he was the one who got us all organized when everyone else fell apart at the sight of the body."

"Exactly," said Alistair. "I've seen a good many dead men in my time, but even so, what was left of that poor bastard's face stopped me in my tracks. It didn't throw Richard, though. He was right there, examining the body and cracking out orders. It's not natural, Jamie. And when I asked him about it, do you know what he said? He said murders fascinate him, so he spends all his time reading about them. Never trust a man who reads, Jamie; it gives him ideas. The wrong sort of ideas."

"Maybe. But right now he seems to be the only one of

us who knows what he's doing. He goes with us. If only so we can keep a close eye on him.''

"I don't trust him," said Alistair. "He's hiding something.''

"Everyone has something to hide," said Jamie. "All that matters right now is finding the freak before he kills again. This is my home. Whatever happened through the years, I always felt safe and secure here. The freak's taken that away from me, and I want it back. I want my home back.''

Alistair dropped a heavy hand on Jamie's shoulder. "Buck up, lad. We'll find the freak and kill him, and then things'll get back to normal again. You'll see.''

Greaves looked disapprovingly at Robbie Brennan as the minstrel helped himself to a second large snifter of brandy. "Look at the state of you. I don't know which makes your hands shake the more, the fear or the drink. The young master will have need of us soon, and he'll be none too pleased if he finds you the worse for drink. Get a hold of yourself, man!''

"Go to hell," said Brennan flatly. "You're a cold fish, Greaves, and always have been. I've never seen an honest emotion cross that cold face of yours in all the years I've known you. It's always been 'yes sir, no sir, can I wipe your arse now, sir?' I've been with this Family for forty years, long before you came along, but I've always been my own man.''

Greaves looked at him unflinchingly. "Is this leading anywhere?''

"When I was a man-at-arms in the Broken Flats campaign, I saw more dead men than you could imagine in your worst nightmare. I saw them cut down and ripped apart and piled up in huge heaps under the midday sun, and I never got used to it. Which is why I came out of that campaign sane when a lot of men didn't. Duncan would have understood. It's enough to be strong when you have to be. He never expected a man to be always unmoved and unfeeling, like you. So, right now we've got a freak running loose in the Tower, out for revenge on all of us, but I bet at the end of the day I'll still be standing and you'll be crawling on your knees. Because I know when to bend with the wind, and you don't.''

"You always did have a way with words," said Greaves. "But then, that's all you've got left now, isn't it? Your soldier days were a long time ago. Look at you, shaking and quivering in every nerve, with your snout buried in your glass. And Mister Duncan was always so proud of you, and saying what a fine warrior you were on the battlefield. What would he say if he could see you now?''

"Duncan would have understood." Brennan drained his glass and straightened up a little. "I'll do my bit. You worry about yourself.''

"It's not myself that fills my thoughts, Robbie Brennan. And what worries I have are not for you. It's the young master, the MacNeil himself, that we should be concerned about. He had no choice but to reveal the great Secret to all those . . . people, but it must not pass beyond these walls. If it were to get out, the MacNeil would be ruined. It's up to us to make sure that doesn't happen.''

Brennan frowned. "Just what are you suggesting, Greaves?''

"What I am suggesting, Robbie Brennan, minstrel and sometime friend to the MacNeil Family, is that we make sure only those we can trust leave this Tower alive.''

"If Jamie knew what you're saying . . .''

"He is not to know. It is our job to protect this Family, and do what must be done for its safety. The MacNeil is too young to understand.''

They looked at each other for a long moment, until Brennan finally nodded and put down his empty glass.

Holly accepted a snifter of brandy from Lord Arthur, and nodded her thanks. Her hands were steadying, and some color was finally coming back into her cheeks. She smiled briefly around her, and then lowered her head again. "I'm sorry. I'm not usually like this. It's the shock.''

"It's all right," said Arthur. "We understand.''

"There's no need to hover over her like that, Arthur.'' said David Brook testily. "Give the poor girl room to breathe.''

Arthur nodded quickly, and stepped back a pace. Holly gripped his hand firmly, and reached out to take David's hand too.

"Please, don't argue. I'm feeling better now. Let's get out of here. We can stay with friends, in the city."

"We can't leave just now, pet," said Katrina soothingly. "You heard your brother; the wards are up. We can't leave the Tower till tomorrow morning. But we're perfectly safe here. Nothing can get to us."

"It'll be all right, Holly," said Arthur. "I won't let anyone hurt you."

David shot him an exasperated look, and turned back to Holly. "We'll look after you, darling. It's obvious who the killer is. It's that damned freak Jamie told us about earlier. All we have to do is track him down."

"No! That's too dangerous. He might kill you!" Holly gripped his hand hard, as though to physically restrain him from leaving. David smiled and patted her hand comfortingly.

"There's nothing to worry about. The freak doesn't stand a chance against all of us. Isn't that right, Arthur? Marc?"

Arthur smiled, and nodded vigorously. Marc turned and looked at them directly for the first time. "We don't know for sure that the freak is the killer. We have no hard evidence, one way or the other. The killer could be anyone. Perhaps even one of us."

There was a long pause as that sank in, and then one by one the others began looking round the room, their gaze lingering on some faces longer than others.

"After all," said Marc, "What do we really know about each other? Even the most ordinary person can do terrible things, under the right conditions. People you've known for years can become strangers in a moment, transfigured by a single insight or a hidden motive. Who is there you can really trust, when you come right down to it? Some days you can't even trust yourself."

"You have to trust someone," said Arthur. "And better a friend than a stranger. Take yourself, for instance. We don't know a single thing about you, except for what you've chosen to tell us. You could have all kinds of secrets, for all we know.''

"Oh honestly, Arthur," said Katrina crushingly. "If Marc did have something to hide, he wouldn't have brought up the subject in the first place, would he? You'll have to excuse Arthur, Marc; his mouth tends to say things before his brain can catch up. Anyway, I think you're barking up the wrong tree, dear. I've known Jamie and David and Arthur for years, and they don't have a malicious bone in their bodies.

"But Alistair, though; that's different. He claims to be just a distant cousin, but he seems to know an awful lot about Family history. He knows things even I didn't know.''

"I wish the Guardian were here," said Holly. "I prayed for him to come.''

"Yes dear, we know," said Katrina. "But you shouldn't take Family myths so seriously. Most of them are just legends and fireside tales that have grown in the telling.''

"The freak turned out to be real," said Holly stubbornly. "So why not the Guardian too?''

"Personally, I have to say I've got a few doubts about Richard," said David thoughtfully. "He seems awfully full of himself, for a minor cousin from Lower Markham. I didn't even know the Family had branches in that part of the world. What about you, Marc? You ever run across either Richard or Isobel before?''

"Never," said Marc flatly. "Their arrival here was a complete surprise to me.''

"Now, don't you dare start picking on Richard," said Katrina. "Just because he comes from Lower Markham. We've always known that some parts of the Family have . . . gone down in the world. And remember, he's one of the few people to stick by us, even after he found out about the Secret.''

"Yes," said David. "Interesting, that. Why should he and his sister be so loyal? Why come all this way, with winter so close?''

"Presumably, he expects Duncan to make it worth his while in the will," said Arthur.

"Could be," said David. "But that might not be his only motive."

"What other motive could he have?" said Katrina.

"Why don't we ask him?" suggested Marc.

"Yes," said David. "Why don't we?"

But just then Jamie strode forward into the middle of the room and called for everyone's attention, and all conversation died quickly away.

"My friends, I regret to say it, but we can't simply barricade ourselves in here and wait for the wards to go down tomorrow morning. We have a duty and an obligation to find the freak and put an end to its miserable existence."

"But no one's been able to find the bricked-up room for centuries," objected Katrina.

"I've been thinking about the problem," said Jamie, "And I've come up with an idea. Based on certain comments and internal evidence in the notes my father left, I'm pretty sure the freak's cell has some kind of window. Presumably not very large, but enough to allow light to enter. So, I propose we make a tour of the Tower, floor by floor, opening every window and hanging out a marker of some kind, until we've covered them all. Then we go outside and take a look. Whichever window remains unmarked has to be the freak's cell. Shouldn't be too difficult to find the room, with that to point the way."

"It might just work," said Hawk. "It's simple and straightforward. I like it."

"Wait just a minute," said Fisher. "Did you say go *outside* the Tower? I thought we were all trapped in here by the wards?"

"The wards do not become operative until some ten feet beyond the Tower," said Jamie patiently. "And no, I don't know why. The wards themselves were designed hundreds of years ago; I just raise and lower them, as and when needed. Now, if there are no more questions, I think we should make a start."

"Obviously we can't all go," said Alistair. "The women will have to stay here, and someone will have to remain with them, to protect them."

"Right," said Hawk. "And the smaller the search party, the better. No point in risking anyone we don't have to. The freak could be out there anywhere, just waiting for a chance at us. This has to be volunteers only, and people who can look after themselves in a fight. I'll go, for one. Who's with me?"

"You do like to take charge, don't you, Richard?" said Jamie.

"Sorry," said Hawk. "I'm just . . . eager to make a start. But of course you're in charge. You're the MacNeil."

"That's right," said Jamie. "I am. So I'll decide who goes and who stays. Since you're so eager, Richard, you can be part of the group, along with Alistair and myself. How about you, Arthur? Are you any good with a sword?"

"Not really," said Lord Arthur. "Sorry, Jamie, I'm not really up to heroics. But I'll do my best to protect the ladies while you're gone."

"I'd better stay too," said David Brook. "There ought to be one person here who knows one end of his sword from the other."

"I'll go with you, Jamie," said Marc. "I'm fairly proficient with a sword, and I hate being cooped up."

"Mister Brennan and I will be happy to accompany you, sir," said Greaves, stepping forward with the minstrel. Jamie smiled, but shook his head.

"No offense, but I think we'll make better time without you."

"As you wish," said Brennan flatly.

"Don't sulk, Robbie. It doesn't become you. I'd take you if I could, but speed is of the essence, and I think you'll be more useful here. In the meantime, barricade the door behind us once we've gone. Make it sturdy enough to keep the freak out but not so heavy you can't dismantle it fast if we need to get back in here in a hurry. Well, no point in hanging about, is there? We might as well go. Unless there's anything you want to add, Richard?"

"I don't think so, Jamie," said Hawk courteously. "You've covered everything I can think of."

''Then let's go,'' said Alistair. ''We've got a lot of ground to cover.''

There was a quick murmur of goodbyes. Jamie took Holly in his arms, and she hugged him hard for a moment before pushing him resolutely away. Hawk pulled the chair away from the door, listened a moment, and then carefully eased the door open. A quick glance up and down the corridor revealed nothing but familiar furniture and the occasional shadow. Everything was still and silent. He stepped out into the corridor, sword in hand, followed by Jamie and Alistair and Marc. The door closed quickly behind them, and there was the sound of furniture being piled against it.

Hawk looked at Jamie for orders, and Jamie hesitated a long moment before nodding to the left. They set off down the corridor, alert for any sudden sound or movement. Despite all that had taken place it was still early in the day, and the corridor was bathed in bright golden sunlight. From out an open window Hawk could hear gulls keening and the distant crash of waves on the rocks far below. Jamie moved over to the window and draped one of the curtains so that it hung out over the windowsill. They continued on down the corridor, swords at the ready, keeping a careful eye on every door they passed. The quiet grew heavy and oppressive, and Hawk's skin prickled uneasily. He hadn't liked breaking up the group, but he could see Jamie was determined to have his way, so he'd gone along with it. But he still didn't feel right about it.

The last time he'd been in a situation like this had been in the sorcerer Gaunt's house. People had insisted on going off on their own, despite everything Hawk and Fisher did to stop them. Most of them had died horribly. He was damned if he'd let that happen again. But there were limits to what he could do in Tower MacNeil; Jamie wasn't about to let him take control of the situation, no matter what. Richard was a minor cousin from Lower Markham, and should accordingly know his place and keep his mouth shut. Hawk smiled sourly. He'd never been very good at that.

He hefted his sword unhappily as they walked along. With only the one eye left, Hawk's depth perception was shot to hell, and his swordsmanship was only a shadow of what it had once been. It didn't affect him so much with the axe. An axe has many qualities and virtues all its own, but subtlety isn't one of them. With an axe, as long as you can see your opponent, you can usually hit him. And a man who's been hit with an axe does not grit his teeth and fight back, as sometimes happens with a sword wound. A man hit solidly by an axe tends rather more to being thrown to the ground with the impact, bleeding copiously and screaming for his mother. Admittedly an axe isn't much use as a defensive weapon, but Hawk never had believed in fighting defensively. He was much more comfortable with an all-out attack, backed up by dirty tricks. Hawk looked disgustedly at the narrow duelling sword in his hand. If it came to a fight, he'd probably be better off throwing the damn thing like a spear.

He scowled, and then winced as a stab of pain flared up around his glass eye. The damn things always made his face ache after a while. The last doctor he'd seen had told him the pain was all in his mind, to which Hawk had angrily retorted that it was all in the eye socket, and what was the doctor going to do about it? The doctor had recommended a change to a less stressful occupation, and presented Hawk with an inflated bill, which Hawk refused to pay.

The tour of the ground floor was accomplished without incident. The windows had all been marked, and there was no sign of the freak anywhere. The large rooms, designed for entertaining were easy to search, and the open, well-lit corridors offered few hiding places. Jamie led the group up the curving stairs to the first floor, which was mainly bedchambers and bathrooms. Everything was still and quiet, the only sound their own echoing footsteps. Hawk felt like a child sneaking through his parents' quarters while they were out.

The endless quiet and occasional false alarms began to gnaw at Hawk's nerves, but he just shrugged it off and kept going. He had to set a good example to the others, who were all starting to show signs of strain. Jamie was getting jumpy, and showed an increasing tendency to check things twice or even three times before he was satisfied. Alistair's scowl was deepening, and he'd taken to hefting his sword impatiently, as though anxious for a confrontation. And Marc had withdrawn so far into himself he seemed to be walking alone through the empty corridors.

The rooms were lavishly appointed, and would have interested Hawk greatly under different circumstances, but as it was, each gorgeously finished room blended one into another as the tour continued. The first floor passed in a blur of empty rooms and silent, deserted corridors, and they made their way up the stairs to the second floor. Hawk began to wonder if they'd underestimated the freak. They'd all been talking about him as though he were nothing more than an animal, all instinct and ferocity, but that was wrong. The freak was a man, and cunning enough to hide his dead victim in such a way that the body wasn't found till hours after the murder. The more Hawk thought about that, the less he liked it. It was more than possible they were doing exactly what the freak wanted: wasting time trying to find his lair while he planned ways of attacking them . . . or those they'd left behind. . . .

The second floor consisted of servants' quarters; clean and fairly comfortable but essentially nondescript. The only exceptions were Greaves's and Brennan's rooms. The butler's room had a bleak simplicity that suggested he spent as little time there as possible. Everything was neatly lined up and squared off as though for inspection, and Hawk knew without having to be told that woe would betide any maid who moved anything an inch out of place while dusting. Brennan's quarters, on the other hand, were littered with a lifetime's collection of keepsakes and souvenirs, most of them military in nature. There were daggers and swords mounted on the walls, and trinkets and mementoes brought back from a dozen campaigns. Hawk looked them over briefly, and frowned as he realized how dated they were. It was as though Brennan's life had come to an abrupt halt when he came to the Tower; that there was nothing from his new life worth the keeping. . . .

The third floor was storage; endless storerooms packed

with the accumulated clutter of generations of MacNeils. Few of the rooms had any windows beyond the narrowest arrow-slits, but Jamie marked them as best he could, and they moved on.

They tramped wearily up the final set of stairs and stepped out onto the open battlements. Hawk took a deep breath as the cold wind hit him, blowing away the cobwebs of fatigue from his mind. The view was magnificent, from the dark labyrinthine sprawl of Haven to the great jagged cliffs that surrounded it, to the vast expanse of the open sea. Gulls hung on the sky far above them, keening on the rising wind like lost souls banned from heaven or hell. Hawk felt he could stand there forever, just drinking in the view.

Alistair stared about him with obvious nostalgia, while Jamie was predictably blasé, having seen it all before. Marc, on the other hand, looked once at the sea and the cliffs, and turned away, apparently uninterested. And then he looked out over Haven, and couldn't tear his gaze away. Hawk shrugged inwardly. No accounting for taste.

Finally Jamie led them back down through the Tower to the ground floor. There was still no sign of the freak anywhere, and Hawk could sense they were all beginning to relax a little. The general feeling seemed to be that the freak would have attacked them by now if he was going to. Hawk distrusted the feeling. The freak was up to something, he was sure of it; something so obvious Hawk couldn't see it for looking. It was as though the freak didn't care whether they found his lair or not . . . which would seem to suggest he'd found a better place to hide. Hawk scowled ferociously and chewed at his lower lip as Jamie led them through the entrance hall and out the main door.

The gusting wind caught Hawk's attention again, and he looked around him. Even after the unobscured view from the battlements, he'd still been half expecting to see some shimmering mystical barrier cutting the Tower off from the rest of the world, but everything seemed perfectly normal. The cliff edge stretched away before him, and the wind ruffled the long grass on either side of the trail that led back down to Haven. A sudden thought struck him. He only had

Jamie's word for it that the wards were actually there. If by some chance Jamie himself was the spy's contact, what better way to draw attention away from himself and Fenris than by concocting the story of the murderous freak? Or could Jamie be Fenris? Either way, it would explain why the spy had headed straight for Tower MacNeil.

But, on the other hand, if the freak was real and the wards were real, that would have thrown the spy completely off balance. Being trapped in the Tower by the wards would have been the last thing he'd expected. He'd have to be getting pretty desperate by now. And desperate men make mistakes. Hawk pursed his lips thoughtfully. So, it all came down to whether the wards were actually there. Either way, the answer to that question would tell him something important. Unless Fenris had let the freak out for some reason. . . . Hawk decided he wasn't going to think about it any more for a while. It was all getting too complicated. All that mattered for the moment was checking whether the wards were actually there. He walked casually forward. He hadn't made half a dozen steps before Jamie called urgently after him, and came running up behind him to grab him by the arm.

"Don't go near the wards, Richard, it isn't safe." He bent down, picked up a clump of grass and threw it forward. It flew a few feet and then flared up suddenly, burning soundlessly with a brilliant, eye-searing flame. Within seconds there were only a few particles of ash, which were carried away on the wind. Jamie wiped his hands on a handkerchief, then tucked it neatly away in his sleeve. "Sorry about that, Richard. I should have warned you."

"That's all right," said Hawk steadily. "I wasn't thinking."

They both turned away from the wards and joined the others in circling round the Tower, searching for an empty window. Curtains and clothing and other markers flapped fitfully at the many windows and arrow slits. An excited shout went up as Jamie spotted an unmarked window, only to quickly fall away as Alistair and Hawk pointed out two more. The four men stood quietly together a moment, looking at the Tower and each other.

"Three?" said Jamie. "How the hell can there be three windows?"

"Presumably there are two more hidden rooms," said Marc.

"And with our luck, two more freaks," said Hawk.

Jamie winced. "Please, Richard. Don't say that. Not even as a joke. Things are bad enough without tempting fate. No; whatever those rooms are, they can't have anything to do with the freak, or Dad would have mentioned them in his notes."

"Not necessarily," said Alistair.

"We're wasting time," said Marc. "The quickest way to find out why there are two more hidden rooms is to go and take a look."

"He's right," said Hawk. "We have to know what's in those rooms. One of them's got to have the answers we need."

"Very well, let's go," said Jamie, staring up at the windows. "All three rooms are on the third floor. They shouldn't be too difficult to find."

He led the way back into the Tower and up the stairs, moving at a fast walk that threatened frequently to break into a run but somehow never quite did. Hawk admired Jamie's self-control. It was only the MacNeil's example that kept him from taking the steps two at a time at a dead run. They were getting close to the answers now; he could feel it in his water. He was still cautious enough to keep a watchful eye on his surroundings, but nothing moved in the shadows and the only sound on the quiet was their own hurried footsteps and harsh breathing. Hawk kept a firm grip on his sword hilt. It was all too easy. Somehow, in some way Hawk didn't understand, the freak was leading them around by the nose. They had to be doing exactly what he wanted, or he'd have attacked them by now. It was the only explanation that made sense.

They burst out onto the third floor, breathing heavily from the stairs, and Jamie strode briskly down the corridor, count-

ing off doorways as he went. He stopped before a featureless
stretch of wall, and waited impatiently for the others to catch
up. Hawk studied the brickwork dubiously. It looked no
different from any other stretch of wall. He looked at Jamie.

"Are you sure this is the right place?"

"Of course I'm sure! I grew up here; I know every floor
and every room of Tower MacNeil like the back of my own
hand. For example . . ." He walked back a dozen paces,
and pressed a piece of stone scrollwork. There was a faint
grinding noise, and a section of wall swung slowly open on
concealed hinges, revealing a dark, narrow passage. "It's
one of the old secret stairways; ends up in the library. One
of the more useful shortcuts built into the Tower." He
pushed the section of wall shut with a grunt, and it locked
silently back into position, with nothing to show it had ever
opened.

"Very impressive," said Hawk as Jamie came back to
join them. "I'll remember it if I'm in a hurry. In the meantime, if there is a room behind this wall, how do we get
in? Break the wall down?"

"That may not be necessary," said Alistair. "Look
closely. This particular stretch of brickwork seems more
modern than the rest."

They all looked. Hawk was damned if he could see any
difference, but didn't say so.

"Look for a hidden catch or lever," said Alistair. "Something that doesn't quite fit, or that seems somehow out of
place."

They pressed in close to the wall, running their fingertips
across the bricks and mortar, and staring intently at every
crack and crevice. In the end, Jamie was the one who found
the lever. It was disguised as one of the lamp brackets, and
Jamie had noticed it was a slightly different design than the
ones on either side of it. He gave it a good hard tug, and
it tilted out of the wall. There was a hesitant rumbling of
hidden machinery, and then a section of the wall swung
open. Jamie stepped forward to look inside and Hawk moved
quickly in beside him, sword at the ready.

The room was small and featureless, lit only by daylight

filtering through a narrow slit window. It was completely empty. Hawk scowled and lowered his sword as Marc and Alistair crowded in behind him.

"Why go to all the trouble of setting up a concealed room and then not use it? That's crazy."

"Not really," said Jamie, taking a few steps into the room. "This was probably meant for use as a last-ditch bolt-hole, in times of trouble or unrest. There was a time, not that many Kings ago, when the MacNeils weren't too popular at Court. They made the mistake of telling the King the truth instead of what he wanted to hear, and had the impertinence to stick up for their friends, even when those friends had fallen out of favour. The MacNeils always did have more loyalty than sense. Anyway, this was probably intended as a hiding place for guests the MacNeils weren't supposed to be talking to, or maybe as a refuge for women and children if the Tower was ever put under siege. We MacNeils haven't survived this long without learning a few tricks along the way."

"Damn right," growled Alistair. "Never trust in the gratitude of Kings or politicians. They all have bloody short memories when they feel like it."

Hawk nodded politely, disguising his interest. He hadn't known the MacNeils had a history of bad relations with the Court. That might explain why Fenris had gone to ground at Tower MacNeil in the first place.

"This is all very interesting," said Marc, in a tone that implied it wasn't, at all, "But do you think we could please get a move on? We have two more rooms to find, and the less time we spend on our own up here, the better."

"The lad's right," said Alistair. "We've left the women alone too long as it is."

"They're protected," said Jamie. "They'll be all right till we get back."

Alistair sniffed. "Some protection; a dandy, a drunk, and two old men. There's no telling what might have happened while we've been gallivanting about up here."

"Then let's stop wasting time arguing and look for the other two rooms," said Hawk, cutting in quickly to head off the row before it got out of hand. ''Jamie, is there a tool cupboard, or something like that up here?''

''Of course,'' said Jamie stiffly. ''Why?''

''Well, it just occurred to me that we might not be able to find the hidden mechanisms for the other two rooms, and we might have to get into them the hard way—with sledge-hammers and crowbars.''

''Good thinking,'' said Alistair, nodding approvingly. ''Well, Jamie?''

''This way,'' said the MacNeil. He stepped out of the room and started off down the corridor. ''Leave the door open,'' he said over his shoulder. ''We might need to find the room again in a hurry.''

They found the tool cupboard easily enough, but sorting through the contents took some time. Jamie had never actually looked into it before—that was what servants were for—and he found the contents fascinating, discovering all kinds of things he didn't know he had. He rummaged away happily, while everyone else helped themselves to what they wanted. Alistair and Marc both chose crowbars, hefting them with obvious unfamiliarity, while Hawk went straight for a short-handled sledgehammer with a large flat head. He liked the feel and weight of it. It reminded him of his axe. He swung it easily a few times, and stuck it through his belt. Everyone then had to wait while Jamie searched for a hammer just like Hawk's. He swung it a few times, raised an eyebrow at the weight, and then led the way back down the corridor to the next hidden room.

The hallway grew darker as they moved along. The Tower's architects had seen no reason to waste expensive glass windows on a storage level used mainly by servants, and had mostly made do with arrow slits. There were lamp brackets on the walls at regular intervals, but with all the servants gone, none of the lamps was lit. The group moved from one pool of light to another, plunged occasionally into gloom as clouds passed before the sun, cutting off the daylight. Hawk peered watchfully about him, his free hand resting on the hammer head.

The second stretch of brickwork Jamie indicated looked

just as innocuous as the first. Hawk tried all the lamp brackets in the vicinity, but nothing happened. A thorough search of the bricks and mortar failed to turn up any other hidden catches or levers, so they did it the hard way. Hawk and Jamie rolled up their sleeves, Jamie clumsily following Hawk's example, and then they set to work with their sledgehammers on what looked like the weakest spot. The old brickwork gave way surprisingly easily, and they soon opened up a hole big enough for Alistair and Marc to work on with their crowbars while Hawk and Jamie took a rest. When the hole looked big enough, everyone stepped back to let Jamie peer into the gloom beyond.

"Well?" said Marc. "What's in there?"

"Looks like a . . . writing desk," said Jamie. "There are papers on it. I've got to get in there. We'll have to widen the hole some more."

He stepped back, and between them the group knocked and levered away bricks until the hole was big enough for Jamie to squeeze through. Hawk clambered through after him, and then quickly turned to stop Marc and Alistair following him.

"You'd better stay where you are; this looks like a really bad place to be cornered in. Watch the corridor. We'll yell out if we find anything interesting."

Alistair sniffed and turned away, his back radiating disapproval. Marc just nodded and turned away. Hawk moved over to join Jamie, who was leaning over the desk, shuffling through a sheaf of papers and squinting at them in the meager light from the slit window. There was a lamp on the desk. Hawk picked it up and shook it, and heard oil gurgle. He raised an eyebrow. Someone had been in the room recently. Which meant there was a way in that they'd missed. He shrugged and lit the lamp, holding it over the papers. The crabbed handwriting was difficult to read, even with the additional light, but Hawk was able to make out enough of it to give him goose flesh. The author had to be the freaks's father. Jamie swore softly as he struggled with the handwriting.

"These are old, Richard, really old. I need to study them.

This bit here seems to have been written directly after the freak was walled up and left to die; something about its . . . unnatural appetites. There are hints here about what the freak actually is, and how to deal with it; all the things Dad never got around to telling me. Richard, we've struck gold!''

"Don't get too excited yet," said Hawk, keeping his voice low. "Here's something else for you to think about: Someone was in here before us, not long ago."

Jamie looked at him sharply. "How can you tell?"

"There was fresh oil in this lamp. What worries me is how he got in."

"Presumably there's a secret mechanism here somewhere, and we missed it."

"Maybe. And maybe there isn't, and our visitor used magic."

They looked at each other for a long moment. "What are you saying?" said Jamie finally.

"I'm not sure. But if there is a secret magic-user here in Tower MacNeil, that could complicate the hell out of things."

Jamie frowned. "Dad was the magic-user in this Family; I never had much of a gift for it myself. He could have been here while he was putting together his notes for me."

"That's a possibility," said Hawk. "But we can't bank on it. Let's keep this to ourselves for the time being. If there is a secret magic-user among us, we don't want to spook him. Or her."

Jamie started to say something, then stopped as Alistair leaned in through the hole in the wall. "What are you two muttering about?"

"Nothing," said Hawk. "We've just found some old papers, that's all. We'll check them out downstairs."

"Right," said Jamie. He went quickly through the desk drawers, and gathered up a few more papers. He rolled them all up and stuffed them inside his shirt. "Let's go. We've still got to find the third room."

They found it sooner than they expected. They rounded a curve in the corridor, and stopped dead in their tracks as they saw a great hole in the wall and debris scattered across the floor. Jagged half-bricks jutted from the sides of the hole like broken teeth, and the wall itself bowed slightly outwards into the corridor, as though there'd been an explosion in the room beyond.

"That's not possible," said Jamie. "We passed this way less than half an hour ago, and there was no trace of this then!"

"It's here now," said Hawk. He knelt down among the rubble and examined it closely in the light of the lamp he'd brought with him from the last room. "This happened some time ago. There's a layer of dust here that hasn't been disturbed. But you're right, Jamie; we did come this way before. You can see our footprints in the dust over there. Strange. There isn't this much dust anywhere else on this floor."

"What does that mean?" said Jamie.

Hawk shrugged. "Beats me. Maybe the servants just didn't feel like dusting this particular bit of corridor for some reason." He got to his feet, and moved over to inspect the broken wall. "This is interesting, too. Look at the way the bricks splay outwards. They must have been hit from the other side, from inside the room. The freak did this himself, presumably with his bare hands."

"Gods save us," said Jamie. "What kind of monster is it?"

Alistair moved over to study the hole, scowling thoughtfully. "Nothing human could have done this. The wall was stout and heavy, built to last." He peered through the hole at the room beyond, and his voice changed. "Richard, bring that lamp over here, would you?"

Hawk did so, and the others crowded round so they could all see into the hidden room. Scattered across the floor of the tiny cell were hundreds of small bones. Among them were the bodies of several small creatures, rats and mice and other things too decayed and corrupt to identify. The room stank of age and decay, like a freshly opened tomb.

"Well, now we know what he ate," said Jamie, his voice too steady to be natural.

"It doesn't explain how they got into a bricked-up room,"

said Hawk. "Besides, some of the less decayed bodies look practically untouched."

He stepped back from the hole to get some fresh air, and the others gladly took this as an excuse to do the same. They looked at each other for a while, at a loss for words. Hawk nudged a brick on the floor with his foot, and the sudden grating sound seemed very loud.

"Perhaps there's something in the papers that will explain this," said Jamie finally. "I'll check them when we get downstairs."

"There's only one explanation," said Alistair. "Magic. Some kind of illusion. The hole in the wall was there all the time, and we walked right past it without seeing it. Hell, we must have been practically stumbling over the rubble."

"So what happened to the illusion?" said Hawk. "Why are we able to see the hole now?"

"Perhaps we're being allowed to see it." said Marc. "Perhaps the freak doesn't need to hide it from us any longer."

They all looked at him. "You mean the freak knows we're here, and what we're doing?" said Jamie.

"Haven't you felt you were being watched?" said Marc. "Haven't you had that feeling right from the start?"

"The freak must be a magic-user of some kind," said Alistair. "He set up the illusion after he broke out; first so that the servants wouldn't see the hole, and then so that we wouldn't . . . until he wanted us to. Now he's hiding behind another illusion, dogging us from one floor to another and laughing at us all the while."

"Oh great," said Hawk. "Not only is he inhumanly strong and a killer, but he can mess with our minds as well."

They stood quietly for a while, staring into the creature's cell, because it was easier than looking at each other and admitting they didn't know what to do next. Marc finally broke the silence, his voice soft and reflective.

"Think what he must have endured, shut up in that tiny cell for years on end. No way to measure time, save by the passing of day into night and night into day. No sound save his own voice, no company save his own thoughts. And all

the years passing, one into another . . . Did he ever understand why he'd been shut away and left to die, except as a
punishment for being . . . different? Perhaps in the end that's
what kept him alive so long; a slow-burning fuse of hatred,
waiting for a chance at revenge.''

"Don't start feeling sorry for the creature,'' said Alistair.
"He's already killed one man. And he would undoubtedly
kill you, given the chance.''

"We don't know the freak is the murderer,'' said Marc.
"There's no evidence, no proof; nothing to tie him directly
to the killing. For all we know, one of us may be the
murderer, for reasons of his own.''

Hawk studied him thoughtfully but said nothing.

"We can discuss this better downstairs,'' said Jamie, with
just enough of an edge to his voice to make it clear that this
was an order and not a suggestion. "It's obvious the freak
isn't using his cell anymore, so there's no point in hanging
around here. We've been gone a long time. The others will
be worried about us.''

He turned his back on the gaping hole in the wall, and
started off down the corridor, followed by the others. They
made their way silently back down the staircase, and all the
way down Hawk thought of the dead rats in the freak's cell.
He'd studied the fresher bodies very carefully, and as far
as he could see, none of them had any signs of a death
wound. Just like the dead man in the chimney.

In the drawing room, after the search party left, those left
behind at first busied themselves stacking furniture against
the door, but that didn't take long. The atmosphere became
tense and strained. No one felt much like talking. Holly sat
with her back pressed against the wall, her face pale and
bloodless. Her hands were clasped tightly together in her
lap, and she jumped at every sudden noise or movement.
Katrina had given up trying to get through to her, and sat
elegantly on her chair, sipping unhurriedly at her wine and
thinking her own thoughts. Greaves and Brennan stood self-
consciously on guard by the barricade. Brennan had an old
short sword he'd taken from a plaque on the wall, while

Greaves was holding a heavy iron poker from the fireplace. The butler's cold features could have been carved in stone, as usual, while Brennan looked somehow larger and more imposing, as though having a sword in his hand had awakened memories of the man he used to be. David Brook and Lord Arthur sat close by Holly, trying to comfort her with their presence. And Fisher stood with her back to the fireplace, watching them all unobtrusively, and wishing desperately for a sword.

She wasn't sure she believed in the freak, but that didn't mean there was no danger. In her opinion there were enough human killers around without having to turn to the supernatural to explain a sudden violent death. It was much more likely the killing had something to do with the spy Fenris. She shifted her weight from one foot to the other, and hoped Hawk wouldn't be long. She always thought more clearly when she had Hawk to discuss things with.

Lord Arthur got up and helped himself to another drink. David glared at him. "Don't you think you've had enough, Arthur? You're no use to us drunk."

Arthur smiled. "I'm no use to anyone, drunk or sober, Davey. You should know that. Besides, to a seasoned drinker such as myself, getting drunk isn't nearly so simple as it once was. As my system grows increasingly pickled, alcohol has less and less effect on it. I suppose eventually I shall reach a stage where alcohol has no effect on me whatsoever, but I hope and pray I shall have departed this sad vale of tears long before then. But whatever you do, Davey, don't have me cremated. There's so much booze in my body it would probably burn for a fortnight."

"Don't talk that way," said Holly. "It's depressing."

"I'm sorry," said Arthur immediately. "How are you feeling now, Holly?"

"Better, I think." She smiled at him tremulously. "Do you think I could have a sip of your drink?"

"Of course," said Arthur, and handed her his glass. "Approach it carefully; it's rather potent."

Holly took a cautious sip, and then swallowed hard. She pulled a face and thrust the glass back at him. "And you drink that stuff for fun? You're tougher than you look, Arthur.''

"Why, thank you, my dear. It's nice to be appreciated."

They shared a smile. David stirred impatiently. "Don't encourage him, Holly. We might need his sword yet."

"If we ever reach the stage where everything depends on me and my poor skill with a sword, then we will be in serious trouble," said Arthur calmly. "I have all the fighting skills of a depressed rabbit. I never was much of a warrior; I always believed in seeing the other fellow's point of view. Preferably over a glass of something. No, Davey; if trouble occurs, I have every confidence that you will defend us nobly. You're the swordsman here."

"That's right," said Holly. "You always had to be the hero, David, even when we were young. I'd be the captive Princess, and you'd be the valiant hero on his milk-white charger, come to rescue me. I always needed saving back then for some reason or another."

"I remember," said Arthur. "I always had to be Davey's squire, even though I was the eldest. I didn't mind. My father was furious when he found out, though. *You're a viscount!* he used to thunder. *The son of a Lord! Try to act like one!* I always was a disappointment to Dad." He shrugged, and taking a healthy sip from his drink, looked directly at Holly. "They were good days, then. When we were young, and the world was so simple."

"You're getting maudlin, Arthur," said David warningly. He turned to Holly and smiled reassuringly. "There's really nothing to worry about, Holly. I'll protect you, just as I always have."

"And I'll do my bit, however small," said Arthur. "I would defend you with my life, Holly."

Holly smiled genuinely for the first time, and reached out to clasp each of them by the hand. "I feel so safe with you two here. My guardians."

"They've been gone too long," said Katrina suddenly. "It shouldn't take this long to check a few windows. Do you suppose something's happened to them?"

"It's too early to start panicking," said Fisher. "They haven't been gone an hour yet."

"Is that all?" said Holly. "It seems longer."

"It's the waiting," said Fisher. "Time always drags when you're waiting for something to happen."

"It still seems too long," said Katrina stubbornly. "I'm sure Jamie didn't intend for us to be left alone this long. Something's happened, I'm sure of it. I think someone ought to go after them and make sure everything's all right."

"Don't look at me," said Arthur. "I may be drunk, but I'm not crazy."

"Damn right," said Fisher. "No one is to go off on their own. It isn't safe."

"Who the hell do you think you are, giving everyone orders?" said Katrina angrily. "Hold your tongue, and remember your place. David, if Arthur hasn't the courage to go, I'm sure you'll . . ."

"Not this time, Katrina," said David firmly. "For once, I find myself in agreement with Arthur. If the freak is roaming about out there, a man on his own would make a perfect target. And no, you can't send one of the servants, either."

"Thank you, sir," said Greaves. Brennan grinned.

Katrina slumped back in her chair and pouted. "So; we just sit here and wait for them to come back, do we? What if they never come back?"

"They'll be back," said Fisher.

Holly looked at her. "How can you be so sure?"

Fisher smiled. "I have faith in my brother. We've been through a lot together."

"Yes," said Katrina darkly. "I'll just bet you have."

Fisher looked at her with a slightly raised eyebrow, and Katrina decided to go back to pouting.

The trip down through the Tower seemed to take forever. The stairs fell away endlessly before them, curling round and round the inner wall. Hawk's thighs ached from the strain, and his back ached from the tension of constantly waiting for an attack. They were at their most vulnerable on the stairs, and the freak must know it. He'd never get a better chance at them. But landing corners came and went without an ambush, and doors passed unopened. Hawk's scowl deepened. He almost wished the freak would attack and get it over with. But they reached the ground floor without incident, and Jamie led the way back to the drawing room.

Hawk brought up the rear, sword at the ready, his gaze still darting from shadow to shadow. He was beginning to wish he hadn't left the sledgehammer up on the third floor. Alistair and Marc moved close together, also with swords at the ready, almost treading on Jamie's heels. Hawk didn't blame them. It was always when you were nearly back to safety that your adrenalin really began to pump. It was only then, when you stopped thinking about your mission and started thinking about being able to relax and take it easy again that you realized how much you had to lose if something were to go wrong at the last moment. He hung back a little, giving himself room to move, and swept the surrounding corridor with a steady, professional gaze. It wasn't likely the freak would make a move now, after turning down so many other, better opportunities, but Hawk wasn't about to drop his guard just because safety was so near at hand.

Jamie reached the drawing room door, banged on it with his fist, and called out his name. Marc and Alistair moved in close behind him, staring almost hungrily at the door as they listened to the barricade being dismantled. Hawk stood with his back to the door, watching the corridor. He looked left and right at random, careful not to give any attacker a pattern he could anticipate and elude. There was a movement to his right, and he looked sharply round to find Alistair beside him, looking slightly sheepish.

"Must be getting old," said Alistair gruffly. "Forgetting to watch my back, just because I'm nearly home. You'd make a good soldier, lad. You've got the right instincts. You sure you've never had any training?"

Hawk cast about for a convincing answer, but was saved by the sound of the drawing room door opening. Jamie hurried in, followed by Marc and Alistair. Hawk took one last look round the empty corridor, then backed unhurriedly into the drawing room. He kicked the door shut and pushed a heavy piece of furniture up against it. And then, finally, he put away his sword and allowed himself to relax a little.

Holly and Katrina were taking turns hugging the breath out of Jamie, while David and Lord Arthur clapped Marc and Alistair on the shoulder and pumped them for details about what they'd found out. Greaves and Robbie Brennan nodded politely to Hawk as he put down his lamp, congratulated him on his safe return, and set about rebuilding the barricade. Fisher came over to Hawk and offered him a brandy, which he accepted gratefully.

"Any sign of the freak?" she asked quietly.

"We found his lair, but he was long gone. Jamie's got some documents that should fill us in on what the freak actually is. Apart from that, it was pretty much a wasted journey. One bit of bad news: There's a good chance the freak is a magic-user. We ran into a pretty good illusion spell up around his lair."

Fisher pursed her lips thoughtfully. "That's all we needed. Did you come across anything that might tie in with Fenris?"

"Not a damn thing. I'm beginning to wonder if we might have been sent on a wild-goose chase. I haven't come across anything to suggest Fenris was ever here."

"The circle of sorcerers said they tracked the spy right to Tower MacNeil."

Hawk sniffed. "I wouldn't trust that lot to cast my horoscope."

Fisher smiled. "Are you going to tell Commander Dubois that, or shall I?"

At that point, Jamie launched into an excited, only slightly exaggerated account of their journey. Fisher listened skeptically while Hawk enjoyed his brandy. He might not know much about vintages, but he knew enough not to waste a chance at a good brandy. It wasn't often he could afford the good stuff on a Guard's wages. Jamie finally wound up his report, and spread out the papers he'd found on one of the larger tables so that everyone could take a look at them.

With perseverance, and a little discreet elbowing, Hawk and Fisher made sure they got places in front of everyone else.

The pages were faded and cracked, and written in several different hands, running from the time of the freak's birth to well after his incarceration. One writer was definitely the freak's father. The others could have been anyone, from members of the Family to some of the MacNeils' security people. The story that finally emerged from the assembled pages was more than a little unsettling.

The Family could have lived with the physical abnormalities exhibited by the freak at birth. Occasional unfortunates were inevitable when the Quality became as inbred as it had in Haven. It wasn't until the child grew older that they discovered just how inhuman he really was. The freak didn't need food or drink; he drained the life force out of anyone and anything that came within arm's reach of him. At first, no one understood what was happening. When those close to the child felt ill and listless, they just put it down to a bug that was going around. Then someone gave the freak a puppy for his sixth birthday, and the Family watched in horror as he drained the life right out of it. The freak laughed delightedly and clapped his hands again and again, glowing with health and vitality, while the puppy lay shrivelled and still on the carpet.

After that, the freak was kept in isolation. Poultry and small animals were provided to satisfy his "unnatural appetites," but no one save his mother and father ever saw him again. And they were always careful to visit him only after he'd just been fed. The father spent years searching for a cure, almost bankrupting the Family in the process. And then the mother went to visit her son one day, and never came back. By the time the household realized she was missing, it was far too late. His father found him squatting beside her body, singing in her voice. The MacNeil almost fainted with shock when the monstrous child addressed him in his dead wife's voice. It seemed he didn't just suck the life out of people; he took their memories as well. The freak actually thought he was his own mother. For a time . . .

The MacNeil finally did what his Family had been begging him to do for years. He had a secret room constructed
on the third floor, and walled up the freak inside it. Since
the boy was only ten years old, the MacNeil gave him poison
to drink first. It didn't work. The freak lived on, draining
the strength out of anyone who passed by his room. The
MacNeil was at his wits' end. Since he'd already told everyone the freak was dead, and established his second son as
heir, he didn't dare go outside the Family for help. So he
did the only thing he could. He evacuated the Tower, and
left it empty long enough to weaken the freak. He hoped
the freak would die, but it didn't. He could hear it screaming. Eventually, he went back inside and made a small
opening in the wall. And fed his son a rat. He slowly taught
the freak to drain only food that was offered, and not the
person who fed him. It took a long time, but the MacNeil
was patient. And when the freak had finally learned, he let
his Family back into Tower MacNeil.

They couldn't leave the Tower permanently. People were
already asking questions. And they couldn't kill the freak.
His magic had grown as he got older, tapping into people's
minds until they were afraid to antagonize him. As long as
he was fed regularly he remained quiet, and the Family
learned to live with it.

Years passed. One by one, everyone who knew about the
freak died, until it became a Family Secret, handed down
from father to eldest son. Feed the freak what he wanted,
and he would remain quiet. And so it went, down the many
years. The freak lived on, in his cell. Until finally Duncan
MacNeil grew careless, and never got around to telling his
new eldest son. He died in battle, and the supply of living
food stopped. And the freak woke up hungry.

"The rest of it seems fairly obvious," said Hawk. "He
drained the servants to begin with, as they passed unknowing
by the hidden room. Remember the colds they kept getting?
Then he broke out, and drained all the life out of someone."

"The dead man in the chimney," said Jamie. "But why
did he burn the victim's face?"

"I think I know," said Hawk. "But you're not going to

like it. Remember, when he drained his mother, he acquired her voice and memories. Even thought he was her, for a time. I think he took one of your guests, Jamie, destroyed the victim's face so it couldn't be recognized, and then took his place. Only the memories were so strong, after so many years' abstinence, the freak forgot who he was and thought he was the person he'd killed. That's why we haven't been attacked; because one of us is the freak, and doesn't know it.''

For a long moment they just stood there and looked at him.

"That's ridiculous!" said David. "How could he not know what he is?"

Hawk shrugged. "All those years alone must have driven him crazy. Maybe his own personality had become so fragile . . .''

"Wait a minute," said Alistair. "What about the illusion on the cell wall? The freak kept that up for a while, and then dropped it when he realized it wasn't needed anymore. How could the freak do that if he doesn't remember who he is?"

"Maybe he remembers sometimes, when he has to, to protect himself," said Hawk. "How should I know? I'm not an expert on freaks or madness!"

"You're accusing one of us of being the freak?" said Katrina shrilly. "That's crazy! Jamie, tell him it's crazy!"

"Be quiet, Auntie," said Jamie. She looked at him reproachfully, but his face was stern and uncompromising. At that moment he looked every inch the MacNeil, head of the Family, and Katrina subsided, limiting herself to a couple of bad-tempered sniffs. Jamie looked hard at Hawk. "If one of us is a murderer, and truly doesn't know it, how can we tell who it is?"

"Perhaps there's something in the documents," said David. "Something we missed."

"No," said Alistair flatly. "Young Richard has summed up the papers' contents very thoroughly. He didn't miss a thing.''

"We've got to do something," said Katrina stubbornly.

"That . . . creature could be leeching the life out of us even as we speak."

"Has anybody felt ill recently?" said Marc. "Does anyone feel tired or listless?"

They all looked at each other, but nobody said anything. Hawk frowned as he tried to judge how he felt. After the hectic events of the past night and early morning he'd have been surprised if he hadn't felt a little frayed around the edges, but he couldn't say he felt unusually tired. He cocked an eyebrow at Fisher, and she shook her head slightly.

"We have to find the freak," said Jamie. "Find him and kill him. He's too dangerous to be allowed to live."

"Right," said David. "If we don't find him before he feeds again, he could be the only living thing left in this Tower when the wards go down tomorrow morning."

Holly paled suddenly, and turned away. Arthur looked hard at David. "Steady on, old chap. You're frightening the girls."

"Shut up, Arthur," said Jamie. "This is serious."

"Are you sure we can kill the freak?" said Marc. "He's not human. Perhaps he can't be killed by ordinary methods."

Alistair nodded thoughtfully. "You mean like silver for a werewolf, and a wooden stake for a vampire?"

"Perhaps the reason why they didn't kill him is because they couldn't," said Marc slowly. "If that is the case, the wisest thing for us to do would be to lock ourselves up in our rooms, barricade the doors, and wait it out till morning. As soon as the wards go down, we could make a run for it."

"And leave the freak free to turn on the city?" said Jamie. "Hundreds of people could die before he was finally hunted down and destroyed. The Secret of the MacNeils would become the Shame of the MacNeils. I can't allow that. The freak is our responsibility. It's a Family problem. And we have to deal with it."

"Besides," said Hawk quickly, "Splitting up is a bad idea. There's safety in numbers."

"So you keep saying," said David. "What's the matter,

Richard? Can't you cope without someone to hold your hand?''

"That's enough, David!" said Jamie sharply. "Richard's done very well by us so far. Now listen to me, all of you. There's still one source of information we haven't consulted, and that's my father's will. There may be something in the will that can help us, so Greaves and I will set up the right conditions for the reading. It may take a little time, and I think we could all use a break to freshen up, so I suggest you all repair to your rooms and compose yourselves until we're ready down here. But, just to be on the safe side, I think it might be wise if no one was to be left on their own. So choose a partner and stick with them at all times. Happy now, Richard?"

"Not really," said Hawk. "But it's better than nothing. I'll look after my sister."

"Of course," said Jamie. "Aunt Katrina, if you'd be so kind as to look after Holly . . ."

There was a brief rumble of conversation as the others sorted themselves out. David and Arthur paired up together, leaving Marc and Alistair to form the final pair. Neither of them looked too happy about it, but they both made diplomatic noises. Brennan realized he was left on his own, and quickly volunteered to help set up the reading of the will.

There was a pause after that as everyone waited for everyone else to make the first move. Jamie broke the mood by nodding curtly to Greaves and Brennan to help him dismantle the barricade at the door. It was soon done, and everyone set off up the stairs to the bedrooms on the next floor, eyeing each other suspiciously when they thought no one was looking. Hawk still wasn't happy about the group splitting up, but Jamie was the authority here, not him; he couldn't push the matter too hard without arousing suspicions. Besides, he could use the opportunity to talk with Isobel in private. He always did his best thinking when he could discuss things with Isobel. And he had a strong feeling he was going to need all the help he could get on this case.

5

Plans and Secrets

Hawk and Fisher watched closely as the others disappeared into their rooms on the second floor, and made careful mental notes as to who was staying where. You never knew when information like that might come in handy. Jamie escorted Hawk and Fisher to their room, and even opened the door for them. Hawk thought about offering him a tip, but decided Jamie wouldn't see the joke. Jamie made the usual polite remarks about hoping they'd be comfortable, and Hawk made the usual polite remarks in reply. Then they all smiled at each other, and Jamie went back down the corridor. Hawk immediately closed the door, locked it, and put his back against it. His chin dropped forward onto his chest, and he let out a long slow sigh of relief. Fisher made vague grunts of agreement from where she lay stretched out full length on the bed, indifferent to the damage it was doing to her dress.

"I never knew behaving respectably could be such hard work," said Hawk finally. "I've done so much smiling it feels like I went to sleep with a coat hanger in my mouth. I don't know if I can keep this up till tomorrow morning."

"I don't know what you're complaining about," said Fisher unsympathetically. "At least you don't have to be sociable and cope with a corset at the same time. My waist isn't on speaking terms with the rest of me." She sat up slowly and carefully, levered off her fashionable shoes, and wriggled her toes gratefully. "I don't know how women can bear to wear those things. My feet are killing me."

Hawk threw himself into the nearest chair, slumped back, and stretched out his legs before him. It felt good to be able to relax, even if only for a while. The chair was almost sinfully comfortable, and Hawk closed his eyes the better to appreciate it. Some moments were just too precious to be interrupted. But it didn't last. There were too many more important things clamouring for his attention. He opened his eyes reluctantly, and glanced round the room Jamie had given them; just on the off chance he'd spot something that would let him ignore his problems for a while, till he felt better able to deal with them. The room looked back, determined not to be helpful.

It was fairly luxurious as far as Quality standards went; and Quality standards went pretty far. There were thick rugs on the floor, an assortment of classically elegant furniture, and a bed with a mattress deep enough to swim in. Paintings of famous military scenes covered the walls, (military art was *in* that Season,) and half a dozen small nude statuettes smiled and posed tastefully on alabaster pedestals. And over by the window, half hidden by drapes heavy enough to block out the harshest sunlight, stood the room's own private liquor cabinet. Hawk smiled. Now, that was what he called civilized. He started to lever himself up out of his chair, but Fisher intercepted his gaze, and shook her head firmly.

"You've had enough for one day, Hawk. Let's try and concentrate on the matter at hand. Namely, what the hell is going on here? Every time I think I've got it worked out, something else happens that throws it all back up in the air again."

"It's not really as confusing as it seems," said Hawk, settling back in his chair. "It just looks that way because we don't have all the facts yet. Or if we do, we haven't got them arranged in the right order. What's really complicating the hell out of things is that we're dealing with two separate cases here. On the one hand we have an escaped killer freak, disguised as one of us by an illusion, while on the other hand we have our missing spy Fenris, disguised as one of us by a shapechange. We can't sort the two cases out because they keep interfering with each other, and we can't tell which evidence belongs to which case.''

"Could that be deliberate?" said Fisher, thoughtfully massaging her left foot and staring off into the distance. "Maybe Fenris recognized us despite our disguises, and let the freak loose himself, as a way of throwing us off his trail.''

"I don't think so," said Hawk slowly. "The way we look now, our own creditors wouldn't know us. And from the mess the freak made of his cell wall, I don't think he needed any help in getting out. But certainly Fenris could be using the situation to keep the waters muddy. I would, in his shoes.''

"He might know who we are, regardless of our disguises," said Fisher. "There could be a leak at Headquarters. Hell, half the force is on the take these days, one way or another.''

"True. But how many people actually know about us? Commander Dubois, Mistress Melanie, and that sorcerer doctor, Wulfgang. That's all.''

"That's enough," said Fisher flatly. "Whatever information Fenris has, it must be bloody important to have panicked the Council so badly. And if it's that important, it must be worth a lot of money to the right people.''

Hawk thought about it. "All right. There's a chance Fenris knows who we really are. Which means we can't trust anyone here.''

Fisher smiled. "What's new about that?''

Hawk scowled. "I can't believe we've been here all this time and we're still no nearer identifying Fenris. Look: We know Fenris went to the sorcerer Grimm for an emergency shapechange. That means the body he's got now isn't his usual one. Which means we can eliminate all the people here who can prove they've had the same form for more than twenty-four hours.''

Fisher looked at him. "That's brilliant, Hawk. Why didn't we think of that before?''

"Well, we have been rather preoccupied."

"Right," said Fisher. "So, that cuts out Jamie, Katrina, and Holly. And the two servants, Greaves and Brennan."

"And Lord Arthur," said Hawk. "I've met him before. And since Arthur and Jamie have both known David for some time, that just leaves Alistair and Marc." Hawk nodded slowly to himself. "And we've already established Alistair is lying about where he comes from; he didn't know the Red Marches are flooded these days."

"Yes," said Fisher, in a voice that indicated she was about to get picky. "But he does seem to know a hell of a lot about MacNeil Family history. How would our spy know things like that?"

"He could if he was a friend of the MacNeils in his true form. According to Jamie, his Family have a long history of bad feelings with the Court. Which would explain why Fenris made a beeline for Tower MacNeil in the first place. But, on the other hand . . ."

"We shouldn't dismiss Marc out of hand. Do we have any actual evidence against him?"

"Nothing so far. He's a quiet sort; hasn't much to say for himself at the best of times. Doesn't seem to care much for us, but we can't drag him off in chains just for that." Hawk frowned. "But . . . in all the time we've been here, Marc hasn't volunteered one thing about his past; not a single damned thing about who or what he was before he came to Tower MacNeil. Interesting, that."

Fisher shook her head. "Just because he hasn't opened up to us doesn't mean he hasn't talked to the others."

"True. So, for the time being I think we'll concentrate our attention on Alistair, as far as finding the spy is concerned. Tracking down the freak is going to be rather more difficult."

"Why? Once again it has to be someone not well known by the others. The freak might have taken on someone else's memories, but he's still stuck with his own face. So, we're back to Marc and Alistair again. And if Alistair is Fenris, then Marc has to be the freak. Right?"

Hawk shook his head regretfully. "Nice try, Isobel. Unfortunately, it's not that simple."

Fisher groaned. "Somehow I just knew you were going to say that. All right, what have I missed this time?"

"You're forgetting the illusion spell the freak cast to cover up the hole in the wall on the third floor. It's quite possible the freak is still messing with our minds, to make us see someone else's face, instead of his own. Which means he could be anyone. Male or female. And with complete access to that person's memories, there's no way anyone's going to trip him up with an unexpected question."

"Oh great," said Fisher. "So where does that leave us?"

"Wait. It gets worse. It seems to me the freak may be interfering with our minds in other, *subtler* ways as well. Jamie seemed quite determined to split up the group, despite everything I've said, and everyone else just went along with it. Which is rather unusual, considering this bunch can't normally agree on anything without several minutes worth of arguments, insults, and recriminations. Perhaps the freak influenced everyone to accept Jamie's idea, in order to make us easier targets."

Fisher looked at him thoughtfully, still holding her bare foot absently in her hand. "It's possible, I suppose. But how could we tell, one way or the other? And besides, if they're all being influenced, why aren't we? If the freak was controlling the way we think, then this idea wouldn't have occurred to us at all. Would it?"

"That's a good question," said Hawk. "Wish I had a good answer."

"Hell," said Fisher. "I'd settle for a bad one."

Holly sat unhappily in her chair by the fire while Katrina Dorimant studied her makeup in the dressing-table mirror. *Looking good*, thought Katrina contentedly. *Don't look a day over twenty-five. Not bad for an old broad past forty. Graham never did appreciate me, rot his socks.* She smiled. Graham might not have, but there were those who had. Sometimes in Graham's own bed. He never was very observant. She pouted at her reflection. It was all his fault anyway. If he hadn't spent all his spare time and money on his silly politics, instead of lavishing it on her, they might still be together.

She'd told him right from the start; she was prepared to put up with a lot of things from him, but coming second wasn't one of them. She expected all his attention all the time. She wasn't unreasonable; she realized he had commitments. She just wanted him to be there when she needed him. What was so unreasonable about that? Things had been different when they first met. He'd been all over her then, bright and witty and attentive, always ready with a smile or a compliment or an out-of-season flower. When he finally worked up the nerve to ask her to marry him, long after she'd decided to accept, he'd promised her faithfully that she'd always come first with him. Graham was always very big with promises. She should have remembered that promises were a politician's stock in trade.

He'd been so *funny,* then. She missed his sense of humour more than anything. He could always make her laugh, no matter how dark the day.

Still, she hadn't done so badly for herself since she left him. She ran up the bills and he paid them, just as always. And why not? That was what men were for. Among other things. She smiled. Richard MacNeil was an unexpected bonus. Tall, dark, handsome, and wonderfully innocent in the ways of the world. He all but blushed every time she looked at him. She pulled the front of her dress down another inch to show off more cleavage, and considered the effect in the mirror. No, better not. She wanted to attract Richard's attention, not give him a coronary. Besides, it would undoubtably scandalize Jamie, and she couldn't afford to get on his wrong side at the moment. Dear Jamie; so young and already so prudish. Never even had a girlfriend, as far as she knew. She'd have to do something about that, once this nonsense was over and done with. In the meantime she'd do better to concentrate on Richard. He needed . . . encouraging. She produced a small silver makeup case from inside her sleeve, opened it, and pawed thoughtfully through the contents.

"Aunt Katrina, what are you doing?"

Katrina glanced round at Holly. "Ah, you've decided to come out of your snit at last. I thought you were going to sulk all day because Jamie paired you off with me instead of your precious David."

"I was not sulking!"

"Of course not, dear; you were just thinking very hard, and that's what made you frown. Now be a pet, and don't interrupt while Auntie fixes her face."

Katrina removed a tiny black patch from the makeup case, balanced it on the tip of her finger, and pressed it firmly onto the right side of her face, just above the jaw. It was very slightly but quite definitely heart-shaped. Katrina turned her face back and forth, studying the effect in the mirror.

"Aunt, what is that?"

"It's a beauty spot, dear. They're all the rage. And I do wish you'd call me Katrina, especially when we're in company. 'Aunt' makes me feel positively ancient."

"A beauty spot," said Holly, doubtfully. "What's the point of it?"

"The point is to attract a young man's interest. Beauty spots are supposedly there to cover some minor flaw or defect; this intrigues the young gentleman as to what that flaw might be, and how he might get a look at it. Personally, I just think they look pretty."

Holly thought about it for a moment, and then shook her head. "Not really my style."

"Yes, well, at your age you don't need such artifices. Gods, I'd kill for a complexion like yours. Still, at least you're taking an interest in things again. How are you feeling now, Holly dear?"

"Better, I suppose. I'm sorry I went all to pieces downstairs, but it all just got too much for me. I've not been sleeping well recently. I'm sure I could cope a lot better if I wasn't so tired all the time."

Katrina sighed, and put away her makeup case. She turned to look at Holly sternly. "Have you been taking that potion the doctor prescribed?"

"Yes. It doesn't help. It doesn't stop me dreaming. That's why I don't sleep; I'm afraid to. It's always the same dream. I'm lying in bed, in the dark, unable to move, and there's something in the room with me. I can't see it, but I know it's there. It comes slowly closer, creeping towards the foot of my bed. I can hear its heavy footsteps, and its harsh breathing. And I know it wants to do something to me; something horrible. I know I'm dreaming, and I try to wake myself up, but I can't. It starts to heave itself up onto the end of my bed. I can feel the mattress sink down around my feet, feel the creature's horrid weight on my legs. I try to scream, but I can't make a sound; and that's when I finally wake up. Only each night, the creature seems to get a little further before I can wake myself up. That's why I'm so afraid to sleep, because I know that one night I'm not going to wake up in time."

"You poor dear!" Katrina got up and moved quickly over to kneel beside Holly. "Why didn't you tell the doctor all this?"

"I did. He said it wasn't that unusual a dream for a girl my age, and advised Jamie to get me married off as soon as possible. I wasn't supposed to hear that, but I was listening outside the door. Jamie said he'd think about it. But my dream is real. I know it. That's why I began praying for the Family Guardian to come and save me. He's my only hope now."

Katrina's eyes narrowed. "Men! Now don't you worry, Holly, as soon as this nonsense is over I'll see Jamie gets you the best doctors and specialists in Haven. They'll find out what's really wrong with you, and what to do about it. In the meantime, you need something to take your mind off things. Come with me, dear. Come on!"

She took Holly firmly by the arm and dragged her over to the dressing table. Ignoring Holly's protests, Katrina sat her down before the mirror and retrieved her makeup case from her sleeve. She took hold of Holly's chin and turned her face back and forth, frowning thoughtfully as she studied the girl's pale and tired features in the mirror.

"Don't you worry about a thing, dear. Auntie is going

to remake your face from top to bottom. You won't know yourself when I'm finished. Then you can walk into the will-reading with your head held high, and knock them all dead. David isn't going to believe his eyes the next time he sees you!''

"But Katrina, I don't wear makeup. . . . Jamie doesn't allow it. . . . ''

"Oh hush, dear, and let Auntie work. You think about David, not Jamie. I'll take care of him.''

Marc and Alistair sat stiffly in chairs on opposite sides of the room, carefully not looking at each other. They'd taken turns freshening up in the adjoining bathroom, and now they were waiting to be called downstairs for the reading of the will. In all the time they'd been alone together they hadn't exchanged a dozen words. Alistair crossed and uncrossed his legs, and drummed his fingers on the arm of his chair. He glanced briefly at the liquor cabinet, and looked away. That wasn't what he was here for. His Family needed his help, and he wouldn't let them down. He looked round the room Jamie had given him. There'd been quite a few changes in the decor since he was last here. He didn't like them. Too bright and gaudy, by half. But, fashions change, and he had been away a hell of a long time. . . .

He looked over at Marc, who was sitting perfectly still, staring at nothing, his face as inscrutable as ever. Was this what the Family had come to, a cold fish like him? The MacNeil blood must be running pretty damned thin these days. The man looked more like a funeral director than a young blade of the Quality. Alistair stirred impatiently. He found Marc's continued silence intensely irritating. There were things he needed to say, things he needed to discuss with someone, important things; and who had Jamie paired him off with? An undertaker who'd taken a vow of silence, with all the open emotions of a garden statue.

Alistair settled back in his chair and put a curb on his impatience. He shouldn't be too hard on the lad. After all, Marc was all alone and a long way from home. He was probably just shy and ill at ease. He could be waiting for

Alistair to make the first move. Alistair ran through half a dozen possible openings, designed to lead the conversation round to what he wanted to talk about, but faced with Marc's cold visage they all seemed either fatuous or foolish.

All right, then; to hell with being polite. Be direct.

He leaned forward in his chair and fixed Marc with his gaze. "You've been doing a lot of thinking, young Marc. Who do you think the freak is?"

Marc met the older man's gaze unflinchingly. "I don't know, cousin. It could be any of us. If Richard is right, and the creature truly no longer remembers what it is, then I suppose it could even be you or I, and we wouldn't know. It's a frightening thought; the possibility that you might not be who you think you are, but actually someone else entirely. And yet I'm not sure that I agree with Richard. In order to pass as one of us, the freak must be maintaining a fairly complex illusion spell. How could he do that, and not be aware of what he is?"

"I don't know," said Alistair. "But the mind's a funny thing. Maybe part of him remembers; just enough to protect him without breaking the hold his new memories have on him. But even so, we're still dealing with someone who's spent most of his life going crazy in solitary confinement. Even with his new memories to lean on, he's bound to find himself in situations he can't cope with. And that's when his true nature can't help but reveal itself."

Marc looked at him thoughtfully. "I take it you're about to suggest someone you think has been acting out of character."

"Exactly," said Alistair. "I don't like the way Richard's been acting. He's from a very minor branch of the Family, lives in the middle of nowhere, and by his own account has spent most of his life with his nose in a book. But ever since we found the body, he's been taking charge, snapping out orders and generally behaving more like a hardened soldier or a Guard. It's as though he's confused the memories of who he's supposed to be with those of the people he read about. And out of all of us, he's always seemed the least scared. Perhaps because deep down he knows he's got nothing to worry about.''

"You may have something there,'' said Marc slowly. "I've been watching Richard, too. He was very quick on picking up the freak's story from the papers Jamie found, wasn't he? Have you told anyone else of your suspicions?''

"Only Jamie. He won't listen to me.''

"We need evidence. All we have at the moment are suspicions. We can't condemn a man purely on doubts and theories.''

"We'll get evidence,'' said Alistair. "All we have to do is watch him. Sooner or later he'll give himself away, and then I'll kill him with my bare hands.''

David paced impatiently up and down, glaring at nothing and everything, while Arthur freshened his glass with a bottle from the room's liquor cabinet. He'd dragged the cabinet over to the bed, and was now seated with his back against the headboard and his legs stretched elegantly out before him. He watched David indulgently for a while, and then coughed politely. David shot him a glance without slowing his pacing. Arthur smiled at him.

"Do slow down a little, Davey. You're wearing a path in the rugs and making me positively dizzy. Jamie will call us when it's time.''

David dropped reluctantly into the nearest chair, stirred uncomfortably, and then shifted forward until he was sitting right on the edge of the chair. "Arthur, how can you be so calm after everything that's happened? Has the booze finally given up on rotting your liver and decided to go after your brain now? One of us is a murderer, an insane monster just waiting for his chance to kill again. And we're trapped in the Tower with him!''

Arthur thought about that for a moment. "Does it really matter that he's an *insane* monster? I mean, a sane one would be just as bad, surely?''

David looked at him disgustedly. "I should have known better than to expect any sense out of you. For once in your life, Arthur, try to concentrate on what's happening around you! Holly's in danger here. Doesn't that mean anything to you?''

"Yes, it does. You know that. I'll do anything I can to protect her and keep her safe. But right now she's safe in her room behind a locked door. Just like us. What else can we do now except wait for Jamie's call?''

"I don't know!" David shook his head slowly and relaxed a little. "I'm sorry, Arthur. I shouldn't take it out on you. I'm just . . . scared, that's all. Scared that something bad's going to happen to Holly, and I won't be there to stop it. I've always been her protector, even more than Jamie; standing between her and the bad old world. Taking all the knocks and bruises so she wouldn't have to. I'd die for her, Arthur. But all I can do now is sit on my backside and wait for something to go wrong. I just feel so bloody helpless!''

"We all do, Davey. Save your strength. Save it for when it's needed.''

David sighed heavily. "I never was very good at waiting. I've always needed to be doing something, anything.''

"Our time will come. In the meantime, why not have a drink?''

David looked at him sternly. "That's your answer to everything, isn't it? Get smashed out of your mind till the world stops bothering you. Don't you know that stuff's killing you?''

"Sure," said Arthur. "But what makes you think I give a damn? Nobody else does, so why should I buck the trend? It's not enough just to live, Davey; there has to be some purpose in it, some reason to get out of bed in the morning. And I never found one.

"For a while I tried to be the kind of man my Family wanted, but after they all died I lost interest. There didn't seem any point in it once they were gone. I had all the money I'd ever need, and the estate practically runs itself. So, mostly I just settled for having a good time. Believe me, Davey, you'd be surprised how deadly dull having a good time can be after a while. One party blurs into another, the days drag on, and sometimes you think the night is never going to end. I can't seem to get interested in anything anymore. Nothing really matters to me. Except you and Holly. You're important to me, Davey. You do know that, don't you?''

"Of course," said David. "We've always been friends, the three of us. Always will be."

"Friends," said Arthur. "Yes." He took a long drink from his glass.

"You need a woman in your life," said David. "Surely at all those parties there must have been someone, some woman who made your heart beat faster. . . ."

"There was one woman I loved. But I never told her."

"Why not?"

"Because I cared for her too much to ruin her life by becoming a part of it. I've messed up my own life quite thoroughly. I'm damned if I'll drag her down with me. Besides, she already has someone, someone who'll make her much happier than I ever could."

David shook his head. "Arthur, you mustn't think so badly of yourself."

"Why not? Everyone else does. Even you."

"That's different. I'm your friend. All your friends worry about you."

"Friends," said Arthur, sipping at his drink. "I used to think I had a lot of friends. After all, there's no one so popular as a drunk with money. But I had to make out my will the other week. Instructions from the Family lawyer. So there I was, sitting at my desk in my study, and I found there was hardly anyone I wanted to leave anything to. I know lots of people, but the only time I ever see them are at parties. Not one of them ever called at my house during the day to say hello, or ask how I was, or just to chat for a while over a glass of something. In the end, I found there were only three people in my life who I thought might regret my passing. You, Holly, and Louis Hightower. That's it. And be honest now. How many of you would even bother to come to my funeral if it was raining?''

"There is nothing so boring as a maudlin drunk," said David firmly. "If you're just going to feel sorry for yourself . . ."

"It's a dirty job," said Arthur. "But someone has to do it."

"Oh, stop it! Of course you have other friends. What about Jamie?"

"He's your friend, not mine. He just puts up with me because of you and Holly."

"Look, if you're so determined to kill yourself, why are you dragging it out? Do the honourable thing and put yourself out of your misery! Oh hell . . . I'm sorry, Arthur. You'd think I'd know better by now than to argue with you while you're drunk. Just . . . snap out of it. You've got a lot to live for. There's a lot more to life than drink."

"I don't care for drugs," said Arthur. "I'm a traditionalist at heart."

"You're just trying to annoy me, aren't you? Look, you can't kill yourself. Think how upset Holly would be. Now let's change the subject. Gods, you can be depressing at times, Arthur. You're not the only one with problems, you know. I have problems too, but you don't see me crying into my wine over them."

Arthur looked at him steadily. "You've never had problems. You've always been handsome and popular. Your Family bend over backwards to indulge you. Women have been chasing you ever since your voice dropped. You have so many friends your parties often spill over into a second house. What problems do you have, Davey? Not being able to choose which shirt to wear next?"

David looked at him for a long moment. "You know your trouble, Arthur? You're so wrapped up in your precious self-pity you can't see beyond the end of your own nose. Haven't you ever wondered why I spend so much time with you and Holly and Jamie, instead of running off to join the army and see the world, like the rest of our contemporaries?"

Arthur frowned. "That's right. Your Family's famous for its strong tradition of military service, isn't it? Practically obligatory, from what I've heard. I suppose I just assumed you had more sense than the rest of your Family. All right, tell me. Why aren't you in the army?"

"Because the army wouldn't have me. I spent two years cramming with my tutors to get me past the Military Academy entrance exams, two years working my guts out, and I still didn't pass. I didn't even come close. Whatever it takes to be an officer, I don't have it. There was nothing my Family could do. There were all kinds of strings they could have pulled on my behalf, once I got into the Academy, but not even their influence could persuade the Academy to accept such a spectacular failure as me.

"They couldn't even get me into the diplomatic corps, where most of our Family's second-raters end up.

"My father threatened to disown me. Most of my Family aren't talking to me, and those that are never miss an opportunity to remind me how badly I let them all down. And as for my friends, practically everyone I grew up with is in the army now, scattered across the Low Kingdoms, defending our borders. Some of them have already died doing it. And every time I find a familiar name in the death lists I think *That could have been me. That should have been me.* We've more in common than you think, Arthur."

Arthur looked at him unflinchingly. "I'm sorry, Davey. You're right, I should have known, but I just never thought about it. You see, you're the only man I ever envied. Because you've got the only thing I ever wanted. You have Holly."

There was a long pause as they looked at each other. To his credit, David didn't look away. "So it is her. We often wondered, but you never said anything. Holly and I love each other, Arthur. We always have. We're going to be married soon. I wish . . . things could have been different. We used to be so close, the three of us."

"We were children then. Children grow up."

There was a sudden knocking at the door. The two men jumped to their feet as the door burst open and Jamie hurried in.

"What is it?" asked David, as Jamie shut the door behind him. "What's happened?"

"Relax," said Jamie. "There's no emergency. I just needed someone to talk to. I don't know what to do. At the moment I'm pinning all my hopes on Dad's will, that there'll be something in it that can help us, but it's a slim hope at best. I'm not up to this. In the past, whenever there was a problem, I could always turn to Dad. He always knew what to do. Now there's just me, and everything's going wrong."

"Oh hell," said David. "Another one."

"Ignore him," said Arthur quickly. "You mustn't blame yourself, Jamie. You're doing everything you can. We understand how hard it is. It's not easy, learning how to stand on your own feet. Some people never do learn. But you're doing fine so far. Isn't he, Davey?"

"Damn right," said David. "You found your father's papers, didn't you? Without them, we might never have found out what kind of monster we were dealing with."

"I can't help feeling Dad would have done things differently," said Jamie. "He was the great warrior, after all; the great hero. Everyone said so, even the King. I was so proud of him . . . even though I never got to see much of him. He was away with the army a lot, especially after Mother died when I was young. But he was spending more time at the Tower just recently, and we were really getting to know each other. And then he had to go and die in that stupid little clash on the border. I couldn't believe it when I heard. How could he have been so *stupid?* He didn't have to go up there in person, not someone of his rank. He must have known it wasn't safe up there! But he went anyway, because he couldn't bear to miss out on the action. And he got himself killed, leaving Holly and me alone. And on top of all that, he hadn't even bothered to tell me the Secret, as he should have!"

He was close to tears, his face bright red with anger and frustration. Arthur took him by the arm, and gently but firmly made him sit down on the nearest chair. "It's all right to be angry, Jamie," he said softly. "I was angry at my Family when they all died so suddenly, going off and leaving me all alone. But it wasn't your father's fault. He didn't mean to leave you. He just made a mistake, that's all; a simple mistake in judgement."

"Right," said David, sitting on the arm of the chair.

"Everyone makes mistakes, Jamie. Even a great hero like your dad."

"The whole border situation is a mess right now," said Arthur. "Practically everyone I know has lost somebody to one border clash or another. If Outremer doesn't back down soon, we could find ourselves in a full-fledged war."

"It won't come to that," said David. "No one wants a war, at least no one that matters, and no one really cares about the borders. It's just politics, that's all. The diplomats will sort it out. Eventually."

"We're getting away from the point," said Arthur. "Which is, all you can ever do is give it your best shot, and hope that's enough. That's all your father would expect of you, Jamie. That's all any of us expect of you. You're doing fine. Don't let anyone tell you otherwise. Right, Davey?"

"Sure," said David. "We'll find the freak and kill him, and no one will ever have to know about it."

"Right," said Arthur. "Care for a drink, Jamie?"

Greaves looked round the library and nodded approvingly. Everything was where it should be, ready for the reading of the will. Duncan would have been proud to see all his wishes carried out to the letter. The chairs had been set up in a semicircle facing Duncan's favourite desk. The wax-sealed will had been placed neatly in the middle of the desktop, ready to be opened. All it lacked now was the man himself.

Greaves' breath suddenly caught in his chest, and he looked away. He'd known the master was dead for some time now, but somehow the reading of the will confirmed it, made it real. Duncan would never again come striding through that door, to warm his hands at the fire and roar for cigars and his best brandy. Once the will was read, Duncan would become just a memory, a portrait on the wall; and young Jamie would be the new MacNeil in fact as well as name. Greaves sighed. He'd serve Jamie faithfully, just as Mister Duncan had ordered, but it wouldn't be the same. Mister Duncan had been a great man, and Greaves would miss him.

He felt suddenly tired, and sat down on one of the chairs, something he would never have done if anyone else had been present. But it was all right; there was no one to see him. Robbie Brennan was off on an errand, and Mister Jamie and the guests were all safely occupied upstairs. Greaves leaned back in the chair and looked slowly around him. The library had always been his favourite room. Many an evening he had served Mister Duncan and his guests as they sat in the library, telling and retelling marvelous tales of their younger, soldiering days. And Greaves had moved from chair to chair, handing out glasses of mulled wine and dispensing cigars, inventing extra tasks so that he could stay a little longer and listen, too.

The butler scowled, pursing his lips tightly together. It was all gone now. No more evening stories. No more fine parties of great people for him to look after. And the MacNeil himself dead and lost on a battlefield too far away even to imagine, let alone visit. There had been little warmth in Greaves's life as a butler, only orders and duties and the comfort of knowing his place and keeping to it. But Greaves had always thought of himself as someone who might have been Duncan MacNeil's friend if things had been different. And now the man was dead, and Greaves would never be able to tell him that.

The door opened and Greaves was quickly back on his feet, but it was only Robbie Brennan, carrying the extra candelabrum Greaves had sent him for. Greaves pointed silently to where he wanted it, and Brennan lowered it carefully into place. He straightened up and glared at Greaves.

"That has got to be it. We've moved everything in here that isn't actually nailed down."

"The MacNeil was very particular in his wishes," said Greaves calmly. "Everything had to be just so. But we are finished now."

"Good," said Brennan. "I think I've done my back in, shifting that desk. I'd better go and tell Jamie his guests can come down now."

"Just a minute . . . Robbie. I want to talk to you."

Brennan looked at the butler in surprise as Greaves sat down again and gestured for Brennan to pull up a chair facing him. He did so, and looked at Greaves curiously.

"Robbie, tell me about Duncan," said Greaves quietly. "Tell me about the Duncan you knew, in your younger days."

"Why?" said Brennan.

"Because I want to know. Because I miss him."

Brennan shrugged uncomfortably. "You've heard all the songs, but you can forget them. Songs are for entertainment, not history. I first met Duncan forty-four years ago, almost to the month. He was a young officer, the ink still wet on his commission. I was a mercenary out of Shadowrock, serving with Murdoch's Marauders. An impressive name for a bunch of killers, half of them running from the law under names their mothers wouldn't have recognized.

"Duncan and I first saw action together at Cormorran's Bridge. The way the official histories tell it, it was a tactical defeat for the other side. I was there, and it was a bloody massacre. We lost five hundred men in the first half hour, and the river ran red with blood and offal. Murdoch's Marauders were wiped out; only a handful of us survived. The main army was broken and scattered, heading for the horizon with enemy troops snapping at their heels. There were bodies everywhere, blood and guts lying steaming in the mud. The flies came down in great black clouds, covering the dead and the dying like moving blankets. Duncan and I ended up fighting back to back in the shallows. We would have run, but there was nowhere to run to. We were surrounded, and the enemy weren't interested in taking prisoners. So, we made our stand, and vowed to take as many of them with us as we could. No one was more surprised than us when the enemy finally retreated rather than face approaching army reinforcements, and we were both still alive. We were a mess, but we were alive.

"We stuck together after that; we knew a hint from the Gods when we saw one. We worked well together, and slowly became friends as well as allies. The army sent us here and there, and we saw a lot of action in the kinds of places minstrels like to call colorful. Arse-ends of the world, most of them. We fought in twenty-three different Campaigns down the years, and not one of them for a cause that was worth so much blood and dying. Still, we got to see some of the world. Had some good times together. Even had a few adventures that had nothing to do with the army; but none of them the kind of thing you'd want to make a song about.

"Ah hell, Greaves. What can I tell you that you don't already know? Duncan was a good soldier and a better friend. He had a bit of a temper, but he was always sorry afterwards, and his word was good, unlike quite a few I could mention. He brought me here to the Tower, when my soldiering days were over, and made me a part of his Family in all but name. That's my old sword, hanging on the wall there. And you tell me you'll miss him? I miss Duncan with every breath I take. When I wake up in the morning, the first thing I remember is that he's dead. It's like there's a hole in my life that he used to fill, and now it's cold and empty. I should have been there, Greaves. I should have been there with him. Maybe I could have done . . . something. He never did watch his back enough. But I wasn't there, because we both thought I was too old. So he died alone, among strangers, and I'll spend the rest of my life wondering if I could have saved him if I'd been there.

"What do you want me to say, Greaves? That he liked you? He did, as far as I know. Wait until after the will; I'll read his eulogy then. I wrote it myself years ago; just needs a little updating. I'll say all the right things, make all the proper comments, sing his praises and not mention any of the things he'd rather were forgotten. Things that might shock young Jamie and his friends. I'll polish up his memory one last time, and we can all say goodbye. You have to learn to say goodbye, Greaves. It's the first real lesson every soldier learns."

Brennan finally ran down, and the old library was quiet again. Greaves nodded slowly. "Thank you, Robbie. There were many things Mister Duncan could not bring himself

to tell me about his past, perhaps because he thought they
might distress me. But I wanted to know them anyway.
Because they were a part of him. But he is not really gone
from us, you know. He has left behind the young master,
Jamie. There is a lot of his father in him.''

"I suppose so,'' said Brennan. "Sure, he's a good kid.
Is there anything else, or can I call the others down now?''

"We have to protect Mister Jamie!'' said Greaves
fiercely. "He is the MacNeil now. I think I know who our
killer is. He masquerades as Quality, but he does not have
the true stamp of the aristocracy about him. Never mind
who; I am not certain enough yet to point the finger. But
when the time comes, he must die. And Mister Jamie may
not be able to do the deed. He's young, and largely untested.
If he should balk, we must do the task for him. The Secret
must not get out. Or we betray Duncan's name and memory.''

Hawk hurried down the corridor to the bathroom, clutching
at the right side of his face with his hand. He banged on
the bathroom door with his fist, waited a moment to see if
anyone would answer, and then pushed open the door and
hurried in. He slammed the door behind him with his foot,
and made for the washbasin. He splashed some water into
the bowl, and then reached up and carefully eased the glass
eye out of his aching eye socket. He leaned against the wall
as the pain slowly receded, letting his breathing get back
to normal, and then he dropped the eye into the basin. It
stared up at him reproachfully, as though someone had told
it about the problem being all in Hawk's mind. He turned
his back on it, and massaged the right side of his face. He
was already feeling a lot better. When this case was over
he was going to have to have a stiff talk with himself as to
which part of his mind was in charge.

He turned back and studied himself in the wall mirror.
With his right eyelid closed to hide the empty socket, he
looked somehow furtive. Not to mention half-witted. If
someone came up to him on the street looking like that,
he'd arrest the man on general principles. He glared down

at the offending glass eye. The pain was almost gone now, but he had no doubt it would start creeping back as soon as he replaced the eye. As if he didn't have enough to worry about. The case was complicated enough when he took it on, but now things were definitely getting out of hand. Not only was he nowhere near identifying the spy Fenris, he also had to find a magic-using killer freak before it killed everyone in the Tower; whilst, at the same time, keeping the increasingly paranoid others from figuring out that Richard and Isobel MacNeil weren't all they were supposed to be. Hawk sighed, heavily, and fished the glass eye out of the water.

He held it up to the mirror, and then practically had a coronary as he saw the door start to swing open behind him. He crammed the glass eye into his socket, checked quickly that he'd got it the right way round and pointing in the right direction, and then turned smiling falsely to face Katrina Dorimant. She had a hand to her mouth, and was blushing prettily.

"I'm so sorry, Richard, but you forgot to lock the door. I'll wait outside."

"No, it's all right," said Hawk quickly. "I'm finished. You can come in. I'm . . . just leaving."

"There's no hurry," said Katrina, walking slowly towards him. "No need to rush off on my account. I only came in to freshen up. Besides, I've been looking for a chance to get you on your own."

"Oh yes?" said Hawk, in a voice that wasn't as steady as it might have been. He started to back away, and immediately bumped into the wash stand behind him. "What did you want to see me about?"

"No need to be bashful, Richard dear. We don't need to play games, surely; not at our age. We're of an age where we can say what we mean, and pursue those things we desire without hiding behind false modesty. You're a very attractive man, Richard."

She stopped immediately in front of him, so close her bosom pressed lightly against his chest as she breathed. Her upturned face brought her mouth dangerously close to his, and he could feel her warm breath on his lips. Hawk swallowed hard.

"You are a married woman," he said hoarsely, clutching at straws.

"Oh, don't bother about Graham. No one else does. We'll just have to be discreet, that's all. I've seen you watching me, Richard, when you thought no one was looking. Watching me, wanting me, desiring me. I can feel the passion rising within you. Why try and deny it? My heart is beating faster just at the closeness of you. Feel it!"

She grabbed his right hand and held it firmly to her breast. Her skin seemed impossibly soft and warm under his hand, and her perfume filled his head. He thought about calling for help, and then quickly decided against it. If Isobel was to find them like this, she'd kill both of them. Or laugh herself sick. Hawk wasn't sure which would be worse. He tried to surreptitiously pull his hand free, but she had a grip like a beartrap.

"Don't fight it, Richard," murmured Katrina, practically breathing the words into his mouth. Her eyes were dark and dangerous. "You do find me attractive, don't you?"

"Uh . . . yes. Sure. It's just . . ."

"Just what?"

"This is hardly the right place for a romantic assignation," said Hawk, improvising wildly. "Someone might come in."

"We could lock the door."

"They'd get suspicious! Besides, Jamie will be calling us down for the reading of the will soon, and we wouldn't want to be interrupted, now would we?"

"The will. Yes, of course." She let go of his hand and stepped back, frowning thoughtfully. "You're right, my dear; this isn't the right time. But don't worry, Richard. I'll sort something out. Just leave everything to me. And the next time we meet, things will be very different, I promise you. See you later, my darling."

She kissed the tip of her index finger, pressed it to his lips, and then turned and left the bathroom, carefully closing the door behind her. Hawk swallowed hard and slumped back against the washstand. Just when he thought the case couldn't get any more complicated . . . The bathroom door burst open, and Hawk almost screamed. Fisher looked at him.

"What the hell are you so jumpy about?"

"Nothing. Nothing at all. What is it?"

"Jamie's just called us down for the reading of the will. Are you all right? You look a bit flushed."

6

A Dead Man, Talking

The library had been designed for quiet contemplation, or
perhaps the occasional late-night reminiscences of a few old
friends. Cosy and comfortable, a refuge from the hurly-
burly of the world. Now that it was crammed from wall to
wall with several chattering MacNeils and their friends, the
room seemed small and cluttered and not a little cramped.
Hawk and Fisher were the last to arrive, and hung back by
the door to look the place over before plunging in. Fisher
was interested in who was talking to whom, and what that
implied. Hawk wanted to know where Katrina was, so he
could be sure to avoid her, and how many exits there were
to the room. He always liked to know where the doors were,
in case he had to leave in a hurry. You picked up habits
like that, living in Haven. He was relieved to note there
was only the one door. It simplified things. He turned his
attention to the gathering.

David, Holly, and Arthur were standing with their backs
to the fireplace, toasting each other with cups of steaming
punch. They were smiling and laughing as though they
didn't have a care in the world. As though they'd forgotten
all about the dead man and the disguised freak. Hawk
sniffed, and shrugged inwardly. The Quality were well
known for ignoring things they didn't want to think about.
Behind them, Greaves was down on his knees, encouraging

the crackling fire with vigorous use of a poker. He had his coat off and his sleeves rolled up, and looked thoroughly disgusted with the whole business. Presumably in the past he'd had underlings he could call on to deal with such menial tasks.

Over by the desk, Marc had backed Katrina into a corner and was apparently addressing her about something earnest and worthy and incredibly dull. Certainly Katrina's desperation was becoming clearer by the minute as she smiled mechanically and looked past Marc for something she could use as an excuse to escape him. Hawk looked quickly away before she could lock eyes with him, and watched thoughtfully as Alistair took a book from one of the shelves and flipped slowly through it. Jamie and Brennan were arguing quietly about something just behind him, and Alistair was going to great pains to make it clear he wasn't listening. Hawk nudged Fisher's elbow, and the two of them moved over to join Alistair. Hawk had a strong feeling Alistair was keeping something back, apart from the matter of the Red Marches, and this seemed as good a time as any to find out what. Alistair looked up as they approached, and nodded amiably.

"Something interesting?" said Fisher, glancing at the book Alistair was holding.

"Not really, my dear. Just old Family history." He snapped the book shut and replaced it on the shelf. "You're looking very fresh, Isobel. The short rest seems to have agreed with you. In fact, you look quite splendid. Tell me, is there a young man in your life yet?"

"Oh yes," said Fisher. "Can't seem to get rid of him. What about you, Alistair? Do you have any Family of your own, back in the Red Marches?"

"No. They all died some time ago. I've been on my own ever since. But I still come, when the Family calls. As we all do." He looked round the crowded room, and scowled disapprovingly. "Though in my day we came for the sake of the Family, not ourselves. Look at them; gathered together like so many vultures, waiting to see who can snatch the biggest titbits from the dear departed." He stopped, looked at Hawk, and cocked an eyebrow. "No offence intended, Richard."

"Of course," said Hawk calmly. "Personally, Isobel and I will be grateful for whatever largesse Duncan may leave us, but that's not why we're here. We just wanted to meet Jamie and get reacquainted with the Family. We've been out of touch too long."

"A long way to come, just for that. Lower Markham's pretty remote, after all. In fact, I wasn't even aware the Family tree had any branches in that area. Tell me, what branch of the Family are you descended from?"

There was an awkward pause, as Hawk chose and discarded a dozen names, and hoped desperately Fisher would bail him out. It quickly became clear that she was as thrown as he was. Hawk smiled easily at Alistair, and fought to keep his voice calm and even. "I believe we're descended from Josiah MacNeil, on our father's side."

Alistair frowned. "Josiah? I was just looking at the Family tree in that book, but I don't seem to recall . . ."

"Wrong side of the blanket," said Fisher quickly. "That's why he left Haven in the first place. You know how these things are. . . ."

"Oh, I see. Yes, of course. Happens in the best of Families. . . ." Alistair smiled, just a little coldly and nodded to them both. "If you'll excuse me . . ."

He moved away to join Katrina and Marc. Katrina looked openly relieved at being rescued from Marc's monologue. Hawk and Fisher looked at each other, and smiled grimly.

"That was close," said Fisher.

"Right," said Hawk. "If it had been any closer, it would have been behind us. We should have spent more time working out a background on the way here. It's always the niggling little questions that catch you out."

"We can worry about that later. Right now, the day's dragging on and we're no nearer working out which of this bunch is the freak and which is the spy. What are we going to do?"

"Mingle, and keep our eyes and ears open. What else can we do? We can't just drag them off and interrogate them one by one. Unfortunately. We'll just have to keep digging away, and hope somebody lets something slip."

"It's possible, I suppose," said Fisher, looking unobtrusively around her. "They're scared, all of them. Some of them are hiding it better than others, but you can feel it on the air. If the atmosphere were any tenser, they'd be choking on it. As it is, they're all smiling too much and laughing too loudly; making a pretence of enjoying themselves so they won't have to think about what's been happening."

"I don't blame them," said Hawk. "One of them is a murderer, and they could be talking to him right now and not know it. Even worse; they might be him and not know it."

Fisher shivered quickly. "That's spooky."

"Damn right."

"Let's split up, and see if we can get a few helpful answers to some carefully phrased questions. I'll try Alistair again, since he has such an eye for a pretty face. You try Holly and her two swains."

She was already off and moving before Hawk could raise his objections. Lord Arthur might not have recognized him so far, but Hawk had a strong suspicion he shouldn't press his luck. Drunks sometimes had a way of seeing things that other people missed, especially things they weren't supposed to spot. Hawk shrugged, and moved over to join the group by the fireplace. Greaves had given up on the fire and had gone over to try and mediate between Jamie and Brennan, but David and Holly greeted Hawk warmly, and Arthur presented him with a cup of the steaming punch. Hawk blew on it cautiously, and took a careful sip. It tasted hot and spicy, and then blazed down his throat to explode in his stomach.

"Hell's teeth," said Hawk respectfully, when he got his voice back. "No wonder you're all looking so cheerful. This stuff is strong enough to bring a smile to a dead man's lips."

"Thank you," said Holly, blushing. "It's an old Family recipe I found in a cookbook. I thought it might be fun to try it out."

"If your ancestors drank this stuff on a regular basis they must have had insides like old boots," said David, and Holly giggled.

"I don't know what you're all making such a fuss about," said Arthur, draining his cup in easy swallows. Hawk stared at him openly, half convinced that smoke was going to come pouring out of his ears. Arthur just smiled his usual vague smile and held out his cup to Holly for a refill.

"I think you've had enough for the moment, Arthur," said Holly firmly. "You mustn't be greedy."

Arthur nodded and looked at David. "I hope you're not going to let her boss you around like this, Davey."

"Damn right I'm not," said David. "I'm my own man, always have been. I go my own way, come what may."

"You always were stubborn," said Holly, leaning against David as he put an arm around her waist. "But so am I, when I want to be. You needn't think you're going to have everything your own way, David Brook."

"We'll discuss this later," said David, and whispered something in her ear that made her giggle again. Arthur looked resignedly at Hawk, and though he'd been drinking steadily ever since Hawk first saw him, he seemed just as calm and sober as ever. Interesting, that.

Holly, on the other hand, looked quite perky. Hawk thought at first that she was flushed from the heat, but then realized it was expertly applied cheek rouge. At some point during her brief absence Holly had subtly remade her face with a liberal use of makeup. She looked ten years older, much more sophisticated, and altogether more fashionable. Though perhaps not as pretty or as pleasant, if truth be told.

"Well?" said Holly, grinning. "What do you think?"

"Sorry," said Hawk, "I didn't realize I was staring. You look very splendid. Do I perhaps detect Katrina's hand in this transformation?"

"Got it in one," said Holly. "I couldn't believe it was me, the first time I looked in the mirror."

"You look marvelous," said David.

"Very striking," said Arthur.

"Jamie hates it," said Holly, the corners of her mouth

turning down. "He still thinks I'm ten years old. He wanted to send me back to my room to wash it all off, but as Robbie is busily pointing out, the will is to be read soon, and they can't have that without me. Jamie's in a frightful temper. Serves him right for being so pompous."

"Well," said Arthur, after a slight pause, "Only a few moments now to the reading of the will and the great share-out. I take it you're hoping for a suitable windfall, Richard?"

"Arthur!" said Holly, shocked, but David just chuckled.

"Since Arthur and I won't be getting anything out of the will, it allows us to be a little more direct," he said impishly. "Even in the face of sudden death and supernatural freaks, the MacNeils can still find time to argue over money."

"Oh quite," said Arthur. "Still, some of us don't have to worry about inheriting money; not when they can marry it instead."

David looked at Arthur sharply, as though unsure whether to react to the barb or not, and then smiled and laughed and hugged Holly to him. "That's right, Holly. I'm just an unscrupulous fortune hunter after your inheritance! Probably strangle you on our wedding night and flee the country on a coal-black horse! Isn't that what the villains always do in those romances you read?"

"It seems Arthur isn't the only one who's had too much punch," said Holly sternly, though a smile tugged at her lips. "Don't worry, Richard, they're always like this. And I'm sure you'll find Father has left you a generous reward for making such a long journey here."

"Oh, I expect there'll be a little something," said Hawk. "But that really isn't why we came. Isobel and I are both comfortably well off. Mostly because there's not a lot to spend money on in the wilds of Lower Markham."

"I sometimes wish that was the case in Haven," said David wryly. "There are all kinds of expensive temptations here. Right, Arthur?"

"You should know, Davey. I think between us we've managed to lose money in every card game, gambling den, and race course in Haven. I tell you, Richard, not only is

Davey the world's worst card player, but some days he just can't wait to find a horse that's going to lose so that he can put some money on it.''

David glared at him. "This from a man who once bet the deed to his house that he could drink one glass of every potable an inn had to offer!"

Arthur raised a sardonic eyebrow. "I won the bet, didn't I?"

"That's not the point!"

"Boys! That's enough!" Holly looked apologetically at Hawk. "Maybe the punch was a bad idea after all. They're not normally this rowdy."

"You're right," said David. "It's only money, after all. Take our minds off it, Holly, with some juicy titbit of gossip." He grinned at Hawk. "Holly's always up on the latest gossip."

Holly scowled. "I used to be, until all the servants left. You'd be surprised what servants hear. For instance, have you heard about Jacqueline Fraser? Her husband came home unexpectedly and found her in bed with the head groom! Apparently it wasn't just the horses he'd been giving a good rubdown. Anyway, he threw her out without a penny! She had to go begging to her own Family for support. What made me think of that was . . . well, I can't help worrying if something similar might happen to Katrina. I mean, I haven't heard anything definite yet, and Graham's always been very good about paying her bills so far, but he could change his mind tomorrow, and then where would she be?"

"Still here, sponging off Jamie, I should think," said David briskly. "At least she and Jacqueline both have a Family to back them up. I sometimes think my Family would stand by and watch me go under without a single qualm. Tightfisted bunch, the lot of them. Still, bad luck about poor Jackie. I hadn't heard about that. Her husband never did have a sense of humour. You know, it never ceases to amaze me how much there is going on in High Society these days. There ought to be a news-sheet that concerns itself with nothing but gossip and rumour; just so that we could keep up with everything. Maybe I'll start one myself. There might be money in it.''

"Really, Davey," said Arthur, feigning shock. "You'll be talking about going into trade next. I had no idea your debts were so worrying. I'm afraid you'll have to give up your disgraceful gambling habits if you're going to support Holly in the manner to which she's accustomed.''

"I think we'll manage, thank you," said David frostily.

"Of course we will," said Holly. "Stop teasing him, Arthur.''

"Sorry," said Arthur immediately.

On the other side of the room, Katrina chattered blithely on, unaware of how glazed her audience's eyes were getting. Fisher smiled determinedly, Alistair nodded politely while staring into his cup of punch, and Marc's thoughts were obviously elsewhere. Fisher didn't blame him. She'd never known anyone who could talk so much and say so little. Even Katrina's gossip was boring. And then Fisher's ears pricked up as she finally caught something interesting.

"Wait a minute," she broke in, not even trying to be polite about it. "Are you saying Duncan may not have any money to leave? At all?''

"Of course I'm not saying that," said Katrina, her eyes flashing angrily, as much at being interrupted as anything else. "My brother was a very wealthy man. It's been generations since our Family had to concern itself with money. It's just that Duncan was always very careful with money while he was alive, and I don't see why that should have changed just because he's dead. So anyone who came here expecting to get rich off Duncan's death is probably in for a very nasty shock.''

She managed to look disparagingly at all three of them while not looking at any of them in particular. Alistair smiled coldly.

"The fact that you too are hoping for a decent-sized legacy has nothing to do with your opinion, of course.''

Katrina stared calmly back at him. "I don't know what you're talking about.''

"Don't you? From what I've gathered of the way you

treated your husband, it's a wonder he's supported you as long as he has. Your only hope for independence is whatever your dear departed brother may have bequeathed you. Seems to me we may not be the only ones in for a shock.''

For a moment Katrina glared at him openly, her face hardening into ugly lines, and then she recovered herself and smiled sweetly at Alistair. ''I think I know my own brother better than some reprobate banished by the Family so long ago that most of us can't even remember it.''

Fisher's ears pricked up again. She'd assumed Alistair and Katrina had at least known each other in the days before Alistair was exiled, but now apparently Katrina was saying she'd never heard of him before he turned up at the Tower. Which was another small piece of evidence that Alistair might not be who he was supposed to be. . . .

''The money doesn't matter,'' said Marc suddenly. ''What matters is finding the killer among us, before his hunger gets the better of him again. Or has everyone forgotten about that?''

''No,'' said Alistair patiently. ''Not all of us. But it has to be said there's nothing like the imminent distribution of large amounts of money to distract the attention. Let them get it out of their systems, and they'll be ready to concentrate on more important matters again. In the meantime, at least this way we can keep an eye on each other. Ah, it appears Jamie is finally ready to start.''

A sudden silence fell across the library as everyone turned to watch Jamie take his place behind the desk. He looked down at the folded and sealed will, reached out as though to touch it, and then drew back his hand. He looked out at his attentive audience and smiled briefly.

''I'm sorry to have kept you waiting so long. Holly, Katrina, and Robbie . . . please sit in these chairs at the front. Then we can start.''

The three he'd named moved uncertainly forward, glancing at each other as Jamie courteously but firmly settled them into three specific chairs immediately before the desk. He selected another at the front for himself, and then indicated that everyone else was allowed to sit where they wanted. Hawk chose an end seat near the door, only just beating Fisher to it. She sat next to him, apparently relaxed and at ease, but her hand kept drifting back to where she normally wore her sword. Hawk didn't blame her. Will readings were notorious for bringing out the worst in people even under ordinary circumstances. With the freak manipulating their thoughts and feelings, anything could happen.

Jamie moved back to stand stiffly behind the desk, waiting patiently until everyone was settled and quiet. Then he leaned forward and broke the wax seal on the will, and spoke a Word of Unbinding. A subtle, barely felt tension in the room suddenly broke and was gone, replaced by the sense of an almost tangible presence hovering by the desk. Jamie moved quickly out of the way and took his place on the other side of the desk, in the chair he'd set aside for himself. He'd barely taken his seat when the air behind the desk suddenly rippled and flowed, and a large stern figure was sitting where Jamie had stood. Hawk didn't need to be told that this was Duncan MacNeil.

Duncan was a broad, imposing man with a barrel chest, harsh but not unpleasant features, and close-cropped red hair and beard. He was in his late fifties and looked as though he'd spent most of his life in the wilds on one campaign or another. He wore the latest fashion with an uncomfortable air, as though he would rather have been wearing the trail clothes and chain mail of a soldier on the road. His gaze was direct and uncompromising, and Hawk could tell Duncan would have been a hard man to cross. The late MacNeil looked out over the assembled group and smiled slightly.

"If you're listening to me now, then I've been dead for some time. I'm not really here. This is just an illusion, a moment in time recorded by magic, so I can tell you my wishes after I'm gone." He paused, stirred uncomfortably, and glanced at the chair where Jamie was sitting. "You know, this was hard enough the first time, when I made out my will for your brother William. I thought it would be easier this time, but it isn't. Poor Billy. He wanted so much to follow in my footsteps, but he was never cut out to be a soldier.

"Well, Jamie, you're the MacNeil now. I want you to know that whatever happens, I was always proud of you. I should have told you that before, but somehow I never got round to it. We always think we've got all the time in the world for all the things we want to do and should do, but time has a nasty habit of running out on you just when you need it most. I should have made out this will before. Don't know why I didn't. Perhaps Billy's death made me too aware of my own mortality . . . I don't know. Fact is, there are a lot of other things I've been putting off, but I'll take care of them when I get back from the border. Sorry, I'm wandering. Let's get on with it."

He looked down and read from the will in his hands.

"Be it known; I leave my entire estate to my son Jamie, with the exception of certain bequests I shall describe shortly. He shall be the MacNeil in my place, and speak for the Family in all things. Look after your sister, Jamie. See she wants for nothing and marries well. She's your responsibility now."

The dead man looked at the chair where Holly was sitting. "To my daughter Holly, I leave her mother's jewels. She always meant for you to have them. I wish I could have spent more time with you, my dear. You grew up to be a very beautiful young lady, a lot like your mother. Look after your brother. See that he has good advice when he needs it, and when you've got him alone nag him unmercifully till he marries. The Tower always seems a happier place with a pack of kids running loose in it."

"Is that it?" said David angrily. "Jamie gets the estate, and all you get is some old jewellery?"

"Hush, David," said Holly. "Not now."

David slumped back in his chair and folded his arms angrily, while Duncan MacNeil looked at Katrina and smiled wryly.

"To you, sister dear, I leave ten thousand ducats. That's all. Enough to give you some independence till your divorce comes through, but not enough that you can afford to put it off too long. Knowing you, you'll drag the process out as long as you can just to get back at Graham, and I won't have that. I always liked Graham. More than I liked you, if truth be told, and it might as well be, now I'm dead. We never warmed to each other, did we, Kat? Too late now. I don't know whether to feel sad about that, or relieved. Divorce Graham, and make a new start with someone else. Assuming you can find someone else who'll put up with you.''

He turned to Robbie Brennan, and his smile softened. "Robbie, old friend, you get twenty thousand ducats. It's my hope you'll stay at the Tower and be as good a friend to Jamie as you were to me, but if you feel you have to leave, the money should help you on your way. We had some good times together, you and I. I'd have left you a damn sight more than twenty thousand, but knowing you, you wouldn't have taken it. Money always did make you nervous. The Gods know I've tried to give you wealth and position time and again over the years, and you've run a mile from all of them. But I wish you'd take my sword, at least. You know you always admired it, and it's no use to me now. Whatever you do, Robbie, be happy.''

"They never did find his sword," said Robbie softly. "It was lost, somewhere on the battlefield.''

Duncan looked out over the chairs before him, and Hawk felt a chill run through him as the sightless eyes passed over him. Duncan cleared his throat, and looked back at the will before him. "To my butler Greaves, who has always served me faithfully, five thousand ducats. And to every member of the Family who has come to the Tower to pay homage to the new MacNeil, five thousand ducats.

"That's it. I've said my piece. May the Gods preserve and protect you from all harm.''

The air shimmered and he was gone; the last sight of Duncan MacNeil of Tower MacNeil. There was a long silence. Hawk glanced at Greaves, to see how he'd taken being lumped in with the visiting relatives rather than being singled out for reward as he'd obviously expected. The butler was leaning forward on his chair, and tugging at his collar as though he couldn't breathe. His face was pale and sweaty, and he looked sick. He lurched to his feet suddenly, clawing at his throat. Alistair rose quickly from his seat to hold and support him, while everyone else scrambled to their feet. The butler grabbed at Alistair, fighting for air, his eyes bulging from his face. Hawk moved in quickly beside Alistair as Greaves suddenly collapsed, and they lowered him to the floor. His skin was icy cold to the touch, and he was trembling violently.

"What is it?" said Jamie, his voice cutting through the general babble. "What's happening? Is he ill?"

"I don't know," said Hawk, yanking open the butler's collar. "Looks more like he's been poisoned."

"No," said Marc suddenly. "That's not it. Look at him. Isn't it obvious what's happening? The freak's grown hungry again! He's draining the life out of that man while we just stand around and watch!" He glared about him as everyone but Hawk and Alistair backed away from the trembling figure on the floor. "Leave him alone, you bastard! Leave him alone!"

"Somebody do something!" said Holly shrilly. "Don't just let him die!"

Greaves grabbed weakly at Hawk's arm and tried to say something, and then his breathing stopped and the life went out of him. Hawk searched for a pulse in the man's neck, but there was nothing there. He closed Greaves's staring eyes and then looked up at the others and shook his head slowly. Holly was sobbing quietly, her head pressed against David's chest as he held her tightly. Arthur patted her shoulder comfortingly, his face pale but angry. Katrina sat down suddenly, her face turned away from the dead man. Robbie Brennan was staring intently from one face to another, as though looking for the mark of the killer in their eyes. Hawk got slowly to his feet, and Alistair stood up with him, the man's face cold and determined.

"This has gone on long enough," he said roughly, his words clipped short by barely controlled rage. "I'm damned if I'll lose anyone else to the freak. I've kept my peace till now because I wanted to be sure before I made any accusations, but I can't keep quiet any longer. If I'd spoken out before, maybe Greaves would still be alive.''

David gently pushed Holly away from him, and his hand dropped to his sword belt. ''Are you saying you think you know who the imposter is?''

''Out with it,'' said Jamie sharply. ''If you've any evidence against one of us, I want to hear it.''

''Greaves knew who the freak was,'' said Brennan. ''He told me earlier that someone here wasn't the aristocrat they pretended to be. He didn't give me a name, though.''

''And that's why he died,'' said Alistair. ''The freak wanted him dead before he could identify our imposter. But I'll give you a name: Richard MacNeil.''

There was a flurry of shocked gasps and curses as everyone backed quickly away from Hawk, except for Fisher who stayed at his side, and Alistair, who stood facing him. Hawk stood very still, careful to keep his face composed and his voice even.

''I'm not the freak, Alistair. There's no evidence against me, and you know it.''

''Get away from him, Isobel,'' said Jamie.

''You're all crazy!'' said Fisher. ''He isn't the freak!''

''You can't be sure,'' said Katrina. ''Even the freak himself doesn't know who he is.''

''Get away from him, Isobel,'' said Alistair.

''In case you've all forgotten,'' said Hawk tightly, ''May I remind you that the man we found in the chimney had been dead for some time, long before Isobel and I got here.''

''We don't know when he died for sure,'' said Robbie Brennan. ''You're not a doctor. Whatever else you are.''

''Besides,'' said David, ''the freak could have killed the real Richard soon after he got here and taken his place, so as to throw us off the track after the first murder.''

''There's too many *ifs* and *maybes*,'' said Jamie. ''We need evidence.''

''All right,'' said Alistair. ''You want evidence? How about this: He's lied to us constantly, from the first time we met him. He said he was from Lower Markham, but none of us ever knew we had any Family there. Marc's from

Upper Markham, and he'd never heard of him. Richard claimed to be descended from Josiah MacNeil, but I never heard of a MacNeil with a name like that. And according to the Family History I checked right here in the library, no one else has ever heard of him either. Richard makes out he's some quiet, book-reading type, but he acts more like a soldier or a brigand. Presumably from the memories of someone he's drained. But whatever else he is, he's not true Quality. He doesn't know his place.''

"And he was right there beside Greaves when he collapsed," said Brennan excitedly. "Greaves grabbed at Richard when he knew he was dying, and tried to say his name! We all saw it!"

"This is ridiculous!" said Fisher quickly. "Everything Richard has said is true! I ought to know!"

"You can't be sure of anything," said Alistair. "It's obvious he's been clouding your mind right from the start. That's why you've been acting a little oddly yourself. Now please, Isobel, stand away from him. We have to deal with the freak before he kills again, and we don't want you getting hurt."

Hawk backed away, looking quickly around him as Alistair drew his sword. Jamie and David were already reaching for theirs. Hawk drew his own sword, but without his axe he didn't like the odds at all. He glanced at Fisher, who raised an eyebrow slightly and glanced at the door. Hawk nodded briefly, grabbed the nearest chairs and overturned them between him and the others, then turned and ran for the door with Fisher close behind him. There was a roar of outrage as Alistair led the others after them, kicking the chairs out of the way. Hawk charged out into the corridor, waited a second for Fisher to get clear and then slammed the door in Alistair's face. He held the door handle tight, pulled a wooden wedge from his pocket, and jammed it under the door. He'd brought the wedge in case he needed to ensure his privacy, but it was proving its worth now. He ran down the corridor to the stairway and started up it without slowing, taking the steps two at a time. Fisher ran beside him, holding up her skirts to run more easily.

"Where are we going?" she demanded.

"Damned if I know," said Hawk. "I just want to put some space between us and them. We've got to find somewhere we can hide out for a while and do some hard thinking. Our only hope is to prove my innocence by revealing the real freak."

"Not forgetting the spy we came here to find," said Fisher.

Hawk scowled. "I hate this case. We should have held out for a bigger bonus."

"Right," said Fisher.

They both shut up and saved their breath for the stairs.

7

Death of a Lonely Man

For a time there was nothing but chaos and bedlam in the library as everyone shouted at everyone else. Alistair finally got the floor by shouting the loudest and glaring down anyone who tried to object. He stared grimly about him as the noise gradually subsided and a sullen silence fell across the room. Jamie and David had their swords in their hands, and looked dangerously eager to use them. Arthur was clumsily trying to comfort Holly, who was clearly only putting up with him to keep him calm. Katrina had retreated to the fireplace, and was glaring suspiciously out at the room, gripping the heavy iron poker with both hands. Robbie Brennan had thrown aside his short-sword and taken down his old claymore from its plaque on the wall, hefting the great length of blade with professional skill. Marc was still kneeling beside the fallen butler, apparently unable to believe the man was really dead. Alistair looked unhurriedly about him.

"There's no need to get yourselves in such a panic; it'll take us a while to get the door open, but the freak can't get out of the Tower. The wards are still in place, remember? He's still here somewhere, hiding with the girl. If he hasn't killed her already. Finding him isn't going to be easy; the Gods know there are enough bolt-holes and hiding places he could crawl into. But wherever he's gone to ground, we can't just go chasing after him. The cornered rat is always

160

the most dangerous. And knowing Richard, I wouldn't put it past him to have set up some very nasty booby traps for us to walk into. So, we'll go after him, but we'll do it in a sensible, professional way, checking each floor room by room and watching our backs at all times. Anyone have any problems with that?''

Marc rose slowly to his feet. ''We have to kill him. That's all that matters.''

Holly sat down suddenly, her hands folded in her lap like a child's. ''I can't believe that all this time Richard was the freak. I liked him.''

''So did I,'' said Alistair. ''But I didn't let that blind me to his constant lying and evasions. Richard is the freak, Holly; don't doubt it for a minute.''

''Of course he's the freak,'' said Jamie impatiently. ''He ran when we challenged him, didn't he? If he wasn't guilty, why did he run?''

''But then why did Isobel go with him?'' said Holly. ''She swore he wasn't the freak.''

''He'd probably been messing with her mind for so long she no longer knew what was true and what wasn't,'' said Brennan.

''Then why did Richard take her with him?'' insisted Holly.

''Food,'' said Alistair. ''He's woken up and remembered who he is, and he's hungry.''

''If we're to have any chance of saving her, we've got to get moving,'' said Jamie.

''Of course,'' said Alistair. ''But we're not all going. Too large a group would just slow us down, and I don't want anyone with us who can't look after themselves in a crisis. The two ladies will stay here, of course, so someone will have to stay with them, to protect them. Any volunteers?''

Holly looked immediately at David, but he shook his head. ''I've got to go with them. They're going to need my sword. Arthur will stay with you, won't you, Arthur?''

''Of course,'' said Arthur. ''I'll keep you safe, Holly. I

know how to use a sword. I'll die before I'd let anyone hurt you."

Holly didn't even look at him; her gaze was fixed accusingly on David. Marc cleared his throat.

"I'll stay. I'm not much good with a sword, but given time I think I can build a bloody good barricade against that door."

Alistair nodded to him curtly. "I take it the rest of you are with me?"

"Damn right," said Brennan. He was standing straighter than usual, and he held himself with a brisk, professional manner that made him look twenty years younger. "The freak has to pay for Greaves's death. Greaves wasn't the easiest of people to get along with, but he was still a good man, for all that. We were never friends, but I would have trusted him with my life and my honour. He didn't deserve to die like that. I'm going to find the freak and cut him into bloody pieces."

"We won't find him by standing around here talking about it!" said Jamie. "The freak's caused my Family enough heartbreak. It's time to put an end to him. We're going, Alistair; right now."

Alistair bowed slightly. "You are the MacNeil. Just give me a moment to force the door open, and we'll be on our way."

Jamie hefted his sword. "I want him dead, Alistair. No mercy and no quarter. I want him dead."

Hawk and Fisher finally staggered to a halt somewhere on the third floor and leaned against a wall, heads bowed, fighting for breath. Fisher wiped the sweat from her face with her sleeve, and looked back the way they'd come. The corridor was quiet and deserted, the shadows undisturbed. She looked down at her bare feet, and winced. She'd kicked off her fashionable shoes some time back, so that she could run faster, and the cold from the bare stone floor had nipped unmercifully at her feet. Hawk reached up and took out his glass eye, sighed with relief, and dropped the eye into his pocket. The ache in his face immediately began to subside.

All in the bloody mind . . . He looked down at the duelling sword in his hand, sheathed it and sniffed disdainfully.

"If I'd had my axe, I'd never have run. I'd have stood my ground and chopped them all up like firewood. I mean, running from odds like that . . . If this ever gets out, we'll never live it down."

Fisher shook her head slowly. "We can't fight them, Hawk; they're just innocent bystanders. They don't understand what's going on here."

"I'm not so sure I do anymore," said Hawk. "This case has got completely out of hand. Look, there's no point in going any further. The only place above this is the battlements, and there's not enough room to manoeuvre up there. We're safe enough here, for the time being. It'll take the others a while before they can get this far, so let's use that time to get some hard thinking done. We ought to be able to figure out who the freak is by now."

Fisher looked at him. "And what makes you think they're going to listen to us? More than likely they'll cut us down on sight."

"We'll just have to make them listen."

"In that case, I want a sword. I can be much more convincing with a sword in my hand."

Hawk looked at her, amused. "I thought we weren't supposed to hurt them because they were just innocent bystanders?"

"I just meant we shouldn't kill them. Apart from that, anything goes. No one chases me up three flights of cold stone stairs in my bare feet and gets away with it."

Jamie and David made their way slowly along the first floor, carefully checking each room as they came to it. It hadn't taken them long to work out an efficient system. They'd stop and listen carefully at the door, while Alistair and Brennan kept a watchful eye on the corridor. Then David would ease the door open, Jamie would kick it in, and they'd both charge into the room, swords at the ready. Once they were sure the room was empty, they'd turn the place upside down, just in case there were any secret hiding places Jamie didn't know about. Then out into the corridor, and do the same with the next room. Over and over again. The long run of empty rooms was starting to take its toll on their nerves, but Jamie and David stuck at it. Having to just stand and watch helplessly as the freak drained the life out of Greaves had hardened their hearts till there was no room in either of them for anything but revenge.

Jamie still had trouble believing Greaves was dead. The man had been with the MacNeils for more than twenty years; to Jamie it seemed as though he'd always been there. He'd often played with Jamie when he was a child, and been his confidant and advisor when no one else could be bothered to listen. He'd never been a warm man—there had always been something distant about him—but he was always there when Jamie needed him. And now he was gone; dead and gone, like all the others, and there was no one left to tell him what to do for the best. He was the MacNeil now, and the Family depended on him. His Family and his friends. He was damned if he'd let them down.

Alistair kept a careful watch on the empty corridor as Jamie and David ransacked another room. The girl Isobel worried him. Why should she insist on sticking by her brother when it must have been obvious to her that he was the freak, and her real brother was dead? Surely the freak couldn't be controlling her that completely. . . . No, if he had that kind of control, that kind of power, he wouldn't have run from them in the first place. Could it be that Isobel had seen something in Richard that proved he was still who he claimed to be . . . ? Alistair scowled. Richard had to be the freak; it was the only explanation that made sense after all the lies he'd caught the man in. Isobel just didn't want to believe her brother was dead. Alistair sighed, and hefted his sword thoughtfully. He'd have to be careful she didn't get hurt when they finally cornered the freak and killed him.

He glanced at Brennan, who was studying the darker shadows and alcoves with professional thoroughness. The man looked solid and reliable and somehow more alive than he'd ever seemed before. It was as though the man he'd once been had woken up and taken over from the second-rate minstrel he'd become. Alistair felt a hell of a lot safer with this new Brennan to guard his back. Jamie and David meant well, but they had no real experience with blood and pain and sudden death. That was why he let them check out the rooms. Wherever the freak had gone to ground, it wouldn't be in any of the rooms. He was too clever for that. No; far more likely he'd be using one of the old secret passages or hidden bolt holes, waiting for a chance to jump out on his unsuspecting pursuers and pick them off one at a time while they were busy searching empty rooms. . . .

Alistair took a deep breath, and let it out slowly. And swore to himself that when the moment finally came, no trace of compassion would stay his hand.

Hawk and Fisher sat side by side on the cold stone floor with their backs to the wall, as far away from the stairs as they could get. They'd been arguing for what seemed like hours, and they were still no nearer agreeing on anything. There were just too many theories and too few facts. They were after two men, not one, and anything that fit one case inevitably didn't fit with the other. They finally fell silent, staring up and down the gloomy, curving corridor. They didn't dare light any lamps for fear of giving away their position, and the shadows all around seemed dark and menacing and not a little mocking.

"There has to be an answer here somewhere," said Hawk wearily. "But I'm damned if I can see it."

"Keep looking," said Fisher. "We're running out of time. They'll be here soon. There must be something we're missing, something so obvious we're looking right past it."

"All right," said Hawk, "Let's try turning the problem on its head. Assume that all our assumptions so far are wrong. Where does that take us?"

"Right back where we started," said Fisher. "We can't just throw everything out, Hawk."

"Why not? Our assumptions aren't getting us anywhere. Start at the very beginning. We've been assuming the spy Fenris went to the sorcerer Grimm for a complete shape-change, so that no one would be able to recognize him.

Which meant that anyone who could prove they'd had the same appearance for the past twenty-four hours could be ruled out as a suspect. But . . . what if the spy had *already* been to Grimm for a shapechange earlier on, and had just gone back there to get his old shape back?''

Fisher looked at him. "How the hell did we miss something that obvious?''

"Trying to do two jobs at once. This is the first real chance we've had to sit down and think things through since we got here.''

"That's true. But if Fenris didn't change his appearance, then that throws everything wide open again. He could be anyone. That shapechange was the only way we had of separating Fenris out from the pack.''

Hawk grinned. "There's one other way. Dubois told us the spy is a member of the Quality. And like I said at the time, why would one of the Quality want to be a spy? The usual incentives are politics and money, but most Quality don't give a damn about politics and already have more money than they can hope to spend in one lifetime. But one of our merry band here at Tower MacNeil has money problems coming out of his ears. He's admitted he has huge gambling debts, and even more damning, he actually talked about starting a business venture, a gossip paper, on the grounds it might make him money. What respectable member of the Quality would dirty his hands with vulgar trade, unless he was desperate to pay off his debts?''

"David . . .'' said Fisher. "David Brook. You're right, Hawk; it fits!''

"He couldn't go to his Family or friends for the money without admitting he'd made a fool of himself, and his pride wouldn't allow him to do that. The moneylenders would want security he didn't have; he doesn't actually own anything solid until he inherits his estate on his father's death. He was hoping to marry money through Holly, but according to Duncan's will, all she gets is some jewellery and whatever allowance Jamie feels like granting her.''

"Right! That's why he got so upset on her behalf at the will reading!''

"Right. Holly was his last chance. He must have known he couldn't depend on her, and that's why he took to spying. With so many of his Family in the army and the diplomatic corps, he had opportunities to get at all sorts of information. He's our spy, Isobel. No doubt about it."

"Wait just a minute," said Fisher. "That's all very well, but it doesn't help us one damn bit with our current problem, which is how to identify the freak before the others get here. If we can't point a convincing finger at someone else, they'll kill us. Or we'll have to kill them. And if we end up having to kill a bunch of Quality, even in self-defence, that's the end of us in Haven. All the Families in the city would declare vendetta against us, and the Guard would withdraw our immunity rather than openly confront the Quality."

"All right," said Hawk. "Don't panic. I'm working on it. I still think it's Alistair. He lied to us about the Red Marches, and he was very quick to condemn me as the freak. Perhaps he thought he could turn suspicion away from himself by accusing me."

"He was pretty eager, wasn't he?" said Fisher. "And it's interesting that no one seems to actually remember him being banished from Tower MacNeil in the first place. He had to have been a contemporary of Duncan's, so how is it Katrina had never even heard of him?"

"Because Alistair doesn't exist," said Hawk. "He's just a mask the freak created to hide behind. Well, at least now we should be able to sow a few doubts; assuming we get a chance to speak our piece."

He broke off suddenly and looked towards the stairs. They both tensed as they heard quiet, furtive footsteps slowly drawing nearer. They rose quickly to their feet, throwing off their tiredness with practiced ease. They'd be tired later, when they had the time. Fisher's hand dropped to her side where her sword should have been, and she cursed briefly.

"We never did get round to finding me a sword." She reached out and took an oil lamp from its niche in the corridor wall. She shook it and listened to the oil gurgle, unscrewed the lamp into its two parts, and spilled the oil in a wide sweep across the floor. She then threw away the lamp, took a box of matches from her pocket, and held them concealed in her hand.

"Good thinking," said Hawk. "I've always admired your essentially sneaky and devious nature."

"You say the nicest things," said Fisher.

The footsteps grew louder. Hawk drew his sword, and he and Fisher stood side by side. Jamie and David appeared round the curve of the corridor, and came to a sudden halt as they saw their prey waiting patiently for them. Alistair and Brennan moved quickly in beside Jamie and David. Hawk fixed Jamie with his best authoritative gaze.

"Listen to me, Jamie; I'm not the freak, but I know who is."

"Kill him," said Jamie. "Shut his lying mouth."

The four of them started forward, swords raised. Hawk cursed, but held his ground. "Listen to me, dammit! I can prove what I'm saying!" Jamie broke into a run, David only a step behind him. Hawk looked at Fisher. "All right; do it."

Fisher struck a match. It flared up on the first try, and she dropped it into the oil. It caught in a second, and flames leapt up to block off the corridor. Hawk and Fisher backed away from the searing heat, and then tensed as a dark figure came hurtling through the flames. It was Alistair. He stood before them, smoke rising from his smouldering clothes, his mouth stretched in a cold and deadly grin. He stepped forward, sword at the ready, and Hawk went to meet him. Sparks flew in the narrow corridor as steel rang on steel, and Hawk knew right away that he was in serious trouble. Alistair was a superior swordsman, and Hawk wasn't, anymore. With his axe in his hand he could probably still have given a good account of himself, but as it was, it was all he could do to defend himself. He backed slowly down the corridor, using every trick he knew to buy himself some breathing space, but Alistair knew them all, and their counters. He began to press home his attack, his death's-head grin never once faltering. And then Fisher stepped out of the shadows to Alistair's left, and kicked him expertly behind the knee. He collapsed and fell forward as pain exploded in his leg. Hawk and Fisher turned and ran down the corridor.

Alistair slowly forced himself back onto one knee, paused for breath, and then got to his feet, favouring his aching leg. He'd underestimated Isobel. He wouldn't do that again. He looked back, and saw the others gingerly making their way round the edges of the dying flames. He gestured impatiently for them to join him, and started down the corridor after his prey, ignoring the pain in his leg.

Farther down the corridor, Hawk stopped suddenly and Fisher almost ran into him. "What is it, Hawk? Problem?"

"More like a stroke of luck," said Hawk. "I remember this bit of corridor. There's a secret passage here . . . somewhere. Jamie showed it to me earlier on." He pressed hard against a particular piece of stone moulding, and a section of the wall swung soundlessly open. Hawk grinned.

"Grab a lamp, Isobel. With any luck, it'll be ages before the others can be sure we're no longer on this floor."

Fisher took a lamp from the wall and lit it, and the two of them plunged into the narrow tunnel. The section of wall closed silently behind them.

In the library, Holly sat staring disconsolately into the fire. The quiet crackling of the flames was the only sound in the room. Arthur had tried to keep her spirits up with his usual dry humour and amusing anecdotes, but he soon stopped when he realized she wasn't listening. She couldn't seem to concentrate on anything but the thought that David was in danger and there was nothing she could do to help him.

She still couldn't believe how easily Richard had taken her in. Taken them all in. She should have sensed something was wrong about him . . . but she hadn't. Instead, she'd actually found him rather likeable, in an unpolished kind of way. The thought depressed her, and she looked listlessly round the room, searching for something her eyes could settle on that wouldn't require her to think or feel anything in particular. Arthur was sitting next to her, his eyelids drooping, a glass of something as always in his hand. He looked half asleep; either the drink or the strain was getting

to him. Sitting next to him, Katrina glared blindly straight
ahead, lost in thought, the heavy iron poker still clutched
firmly in both hands. Her knuckles showed white from the
fierceness of her grip. And Marc was sitting comfortably in
his chair, a little away from the rest of them, staring thoughtfully at nothing. He seemed perfectly relaxed and at ease,
and Holly looked at him enviously. Sometimes it seemed
to her that she'd never feel relaxed again.

The flames leapt up suddenly as a log shifted in the fire,
and Arthur studied it out of one eye for a moment, before
letting it half close again. In a way, he almost wished he'd
gone with the others. At least then he would have been
doing something, instead of just waiting and worrying, not
knowing what was happening. Maybe it was all over by
now, and they'd found Richard and killed him, and everything could get back to normal again. Or maybe Richard
had killed them all, picking them off one at a time from
hiding, and was now on his way back down the stairs, to
finish the job and silence everyone who could identify him.
Arthur stirred unhappily, but kept his features relaxed and
his eyes half closed. He didn't want Holly to see he was
worried. She looked scared enough as it was.

His hand dropped self-consciously to the sword at his
side. He'd had the same training all young Quality men
went through as a matter of course, but truth be told he'd
never drawn the blade in anger in his life. He'd never given
much of a damn about his honour; certainly not enough to
risk his life in a duel over it. Besides, he'd never been much
of a swordsman, and he might have got hurt. But it wasn't
just his life that was at stake now. There was Holly to think
of. She was depending on him and Marc to defend her if
things went wrong. Arthur's mouth tightened. Probably
Marc would turn out to be an expert with a sword, and he
wouldn't be needed. That was how things usually went. No
one had ever needed Arthur in his life. But if worst came
to worst, and there was only him left between Holly and
the freak, he hoped he'd find the courage to do the right
thing, for once in his life.

He looked across at Marc, and frowned slightly. He

couldn't say he'd never warmed to the man. He seemed pleasant enough, in a dull, earnest kind of way, but basically Marc had all the character of a block of wood. He had no interests or opinions of his own, and absolutely no sense of humour. It wasn't often that Arthur found someone he could feel superior to, and he rather enjoyed the novelty, but there was something about Marc he didn't care for. He was too quiet, too bland, too self-effacing. It just wasn't natural for a man to be that polite. And then Marc raised his head and looked at Holly, and Arthur felt a sudden chill go through him. Marc looked different somehow. He looked . . . Arthur sat up straight suddenly as the thought hit him. Marc looked hungry.

Marc turned his head to look at Arthur, and smiled pleasantly.

"Something wrong, Arthur?"

Arthur tried to clear his throat, but his mouth was very dry. "I don't know."

"You look as though you've seen a ghost. Or something worse. What do you think, Arthur? Have you seen something worse?"

"Maybe. Maybe I have."

Katrina looked at them both, frowning. "What are you two talking about?"

"We're talking about me," said Marc. "It's a fascinating subject, really." He rose lithely to his feet and stood with his back to the fire, smiling easily at them all. "Tell me, Arthur, when did you first begin to suspect?"

"I'm not sure," said Arthur numbly. "Maybe earlier on, when I noticed you never ate anything that was offered to you, and although you always had a glass of wine in your hand, you never drank from it. Drunks notice that kind of thing. And you were always too self-controlled, too unaffected by the things that were happening here."

"Ah yes," said Marc. "Emotions. I never could get the hang of them. Unless you count hunger as an emotion. I'm always hungry."

"No," said Holly, her eyes widening as she shrank back in her chair. "It can't be. You can't be . . ."

"I'm afraid so," said Marc. "And they've all gone off and left the three of you alone with me. We're quite safe in here. No one can get to us; I've seen to that. Or did you never consider that a barricade will serve just as well to keep people in, as well as out?"

Katrina glared at him, holding her poker before her. "You come near me, and I'll kill you, you . . . freak!"

"Such a harsh word," said Marc. "But unfortunately for you, perfectly accurate. I'm afraid I've waited as long as I can, and I really don't care to wait any longer. The others will be busy killing each other by now, so we shouldn't be interrupted."

"You don't have to do this," said Holly. "We wouldn't tell anyone about you. Honest."

"Oh, I think you would," said Marc. "If you had the chance. But I'm afraid I can't afford to leave any witnesses. So I'll take care of you three first, and then I'll go upstairs and introduce myself to whatever survivors there may be. I couldn't do that before; I wasn't strong enough. And the memories got in the way. But now Greaves is mine, the memories are under control, and after I've drained the life and strength out of you as well . . . When the wards go down tomorrow morning, I shall leave this Tower and go down into the city, and I will feed and feed and feed, and never be hungry again.

"I think I'll start with you, Holly. I've always admired you. Like a rose without a thorn; so pretty, so vulnerable. That's why I came to you in the night, while you slept, and took a little life from you, to keep myself going. Your memories drifted through my mind like petals on a breeze, sweet but unsatisfying. Did you dream of me, perhaps? I'd like to think you did. I dreamed of someone like you for years. And now you're mine."

He started towards Holly, and Arthur scrambled to his feet. He drew his sword and put himself between her and the freak, hoping he looked more impressive than he felt.

"Get away from her, you bastard. I won't let you hurt her."

The freak just stood there, smiling. "Very nicely said,

Arthur. Now put away your sword and sit down. I'll get round to you, when I'm ready.''

"I mean it!''

"I'm sure you do. But there's nothing you can do to stop me. As long as I'm within arm's reach of someone, I can drain the life right out of them. Besides, it's obvious from the way you're holding your sword that you don't really know how to use it. Marc knew about things like that, and now, so do I. I wonder what I'll know when I've emptied your head, Arthur. How to mix cocktails, perhaps?''

"Stay back,'' said Arthur. His voice sounded shaky, even to him, but at least his sword hand was steady. He'd often dreamed of standing between Holly and some unidentified villain, being the hero of the moment, but now the time had come and he'd never felt so scared in his life. But he wouldn't back down. Holly needed him. The thought steadied him, and he stepped smartly forward, his sword shooting out in a textbook lunge. Marc sidestepped elegantly, and dropped a hand on Arthur's outstretched arm. The sword fell to the floor as his hand went numb. A wave of shuddering cold swept through him as the strength went out of him and into Marc. He fell limply forward, his face striking hard against the floor, but he couldn't feel it. He tried to get to his feet again, and couldn't move. He would have been frightened, but his thoughts were growing too dim even for that. And then Marc's hand was suddenly jerked away from his arm, and his thoughts began to clear.

Marc fell back a step as Katrina swung the iron poker with both hands again. The first blow had connected strongly enough with Marc's head to send him staggering sideways, but there was no sign of any wound. *Of course not*, thought Katrina crazily. *He's not really there. That's just an illusion of Marc. Behind the illusion, he's probably bleeding like a stuck pig*. The thought comforted her as she swung the poker again, putting all her strength into it.

Marc's hand shot out at the last moment and intercepted the poker, absorbing its momentum with hardly a jolt, though Katrina's hand went numb from the impact. Marc smiled at her, and her eyes rolled up in her head as he

sucked the strength out of her. She collapsed in a heap, and
Marc let the poker drop to the floor beside her. He turned
to face Holly again, and then stopped as Arthur grabbed
him by the ankle. Marc tried to pull free, and couldn't.

Arthur's fingers whitened as he put all his remaining
strength into his grip. Holly needed him. Nothing else mattered. Marc bent down and picked up the poker he'd
dropped. Arthur knew what was going to happen, but didn't
have the strength to turn his head away. He couldn't even
shut his eyes. Marc struck down hard with the poker, and
Arthur's vision disappeared behind a sudden rush of blood.
He still wouldn't let go. Holly needed him. Marc hit him
again, and again.

Holly burst out of her chair and threw herself at Marc,
screaming and flailing at him with her fists. Marc stumbled
backwards and almost fell, but he quickly regained his balance and grabbed one of her waving arms. She fell to her
knees as the strength went out of her, and he smiled down
at her.

"Don't be so impatient, Holly. I'll be with you in a
moment." He bent down and struck repeatedly at Arthur's
hand with the poker. The sound of bones breaking and
splintering was horribly loud on the quiet. Marc pulled his
foot free, threw aside the poker, and turned back to look at
Holly. "There; that didn't take too long, did it? Now I'm
free to give you my full attention."

He smiled slowly. "You know, Holly, you're all I ever
dreamed of, down all the years, locked away in stone and
silence. I watched the light come and go through the narrow
slit of window, and listened to the gulls screaming, and felt
the slow turning of the seasons . . . and dreamed about what
I'd do when I finally got out. At first I dreamed of blood
and pain and sweet revenge, and then I dreamed of the
world beyond the Tower, and all the terrible things I would
do there, and then I dreamed of women, and all the warmth
and kindness and beauty I've always longed for, and never
known except in dreams.

"But the years passed, and the dreams got mixed up with
each other, until I really don't know what I want anymore.

I want you, Holly; you're all I ever dreamed of. So I'm going to hurt you and drain you and hurt you some more and maybe finally I'll hurt you till you die of it, because I want you so much it hurts. Come to me, Holly. No need to be afraid. After all, I'm just one of the Family.''

Holly jerked her arm free from his grip and scrambled to her feet, backing away across the room as he came unhurriedly after her. She looked desperately around for help, but Katrina was lying unconscious on the floor, and Arthur was only moving feebly, despite the desperation on his bloody face. Holly wanted to cry, for them and for herself, but there wasn't time. She kept backing away, and Marc kept coming after her, still smiling. She wanted to scream for help, to Jamie or David or one of the others, but she knew they were too far away to hear her. There was no one to help her. So she'd just have to do it herself.

You're a MacNeil. Act like one.

She chanted that silently to herself, like a prayer or a penance, as her gaze swept the room, searching for something she could use as a weapon. Maybe a brand from the fire; she could set his clothes alight. Except that the fireplace was on the other side of the room now, and he stood between it and her. There were heavy paperweights on the desk, but even as she looked at them, Marc intercepted her gaze and moved to block her way to the desk. She thought about making a dash for the door, but one glance was enough to convince her that she'd never be able to dismantle the barricade before Marc got to her. She smiled humourlessly. She'd felt so safe behind that barricade. . . . Think, dammit, think! She passed by an oil lamp on the wall, and without hesitating snatched it from its niche and threw it at Marc with all her strength. She just had time for a brief fantasy of his being consumed by blazing oil, and then Marc's hand shot up and snatched the lamp effortlessly out of midair. He put it gently down on a nearby chair, and smiled condescendingly.

"Your problem, Holly, is that you keep thinking I'm human. And I'm not. Not really. Why don't I show you what I look like? What I really look like. Would you like that?''

Holly tried to say something, but her throat had clamped shut, and she couldn't make a sound. She'd somehow ended up by the desk, and her desperate gaze fell upon a slim silver letter opener. She looked quickly away again in case Marc had noticed, but his gaze seemed fixed on her. For the first time, he'd stopped smiling. Something stirred in her mind, like suddenly becoming aware of a background noise that had just stopped. Marc seemed to ripple and flow, like something far away seen through a heat haze, and then Marc was gone and the freak stood before her.

Her first thought was *That's not so bad*. She'd been expecting something hideous, some awful misshapen thing, with fangs and claws and bulging eyes, but instead he looked surprisingly ordinary. He was average height but very thin and bony, wrapped in clothes that were too big for him. Marc's clothes. Holly supposed that wearing them made the illusion easier to maintain. Or perhaps it just made the freak feel more like an ordinary man. His left arm and leg were severely twisted, and his left shoulder was clearly lower than the other, but none of it was enough to mark him as a freak. And then she looked at his face, and didn't know whether to laugh or scream. It was a normal enough face, surrounded by long greasy hair and a stringy beard, and flecked with blood from a recent scalp wound, but sometime in the past, the mouth had been sewn together. The heavy black stitches had sunk deep into the lips, compressing them into a thin white line. Holly wondered who'd done it; presumably the father, before walling the freak up in his cell. *And why not?* she thought crazily. *He doesn't need a mouth, after all.*

''How do you speak?'' she said shrilly.

The mouth twitched in something that might have been meant as a smile. ''It's all part of the illusion, my dear. You hear what I want you to hear. But this has gone on long enough, I think. It's time.''

He started towards her, his laughter sounding in her mind. She snatched up the letter opener from the desk and thrust it between his ribs. He grunted once, a dark hungry sound like a pig at its trough, and grabbed both her arms, ignoring the blood coursing down his side. Holly tried to struggle, but all the strength went out of her at his touch. She couldn't even scream as the freak's thin white mouth slowly widened into a grin, the heavy stitches tearing through his lips.

And then a section of the library wall swung open, and Hawk and Fisher plunged out into the room. The freak spun round, throwing Holly to one side. Hawk hesitated just long enough to take in the situation, and then cut at the freak with his sword. The freak raised his arm at the last moment, and the blade cut into his arm instead of his throat. Hawk danced back out of range as the freak reached for him, blood dripping unheeded from his arm. Fisher circled round to try and get behind him. Holly struggled to get to her feet. Hawk stepped in to cut at the freak again, and fell to his knees as every muscle in his body turned to mush. He shook his head sickly, managing somehow to still hang on to his sword, though he no longer had the strength to lift it. The freak reached down and took Hawk's face in his hand. The fingers tightened, and Hawk's cheekbones shifted and creaked under the rising pressure. Fisher snatched a burning brand from the fire and thrust it at the freak's back. The strength went out of her fingers as she came within range, and the burning brand fell from her grasp onto the rug before the fireplace. Flames leapt up as the rug caught fire.

Holly threw herself at the freak, the sudden weight catching him by surprise and knocking him away from Hawk. The freak landed on his back on the burning rug, and flames leapt up around him as his clothes caught fire. He surged to his feet again, throwing Holly to one side, and lurched back and forth, beating ineffectually at his burning clothes with his hands. There was a silent puff of blue flames as his hair ignited. Hawk and Fisher had got some of their strength back, and were on their feet again. Hawk still had his sword, and Fisher snatched up a heavy footstool to use as a club. Holly rose to her feet, ignoring her smouldering clothes, and looked around for something to use as a weapon. The freak turned his back on them and made for the door. He tore apart the barricade, throwing aside the bulky furniture with inhuman strength, and pulled open the door. He staggered out into the corridor, and Hawk and Fisher went after him.

The flames were leaping high now, and his skin was beginning to blacken, but still he never made a sound. He glanced back at his pursuers, made for the stairs, and then stopped as he looked up and saw Jamie leading his party down the stairs towards him. The freak looked back and forth, his mutilated mouth twisted in a snarl, and then his power leapt out, driven beyond its usual limits by hate and desperation. One by one those on the stairs slumped to the ground, their eyes slowly closing as the last bit of strength drained from them, until only Alistair remained on his feet. He advanced slowly down the stairs, his face eerily lit by the flames that still leapt around the freak.

"It's no use, boy," he said softly, so that only the freak would hear. "Your power can't affect me. I'm no more human than you are."

They stood face to face for a moment, staring at each other, and then Alistair's sword shot out and buried itself in the freak's chest. He collapsed silently to the floor, twitched a few times and lay still, curled around his death wound. The leaping flames tugged at his clothes, but did not stir him. Alistair pulled out the sword, and then carefully and methodically cut off the freak's head, just in case. One by one, the others rose unsteadily to their feet as strength flowed slowly back into them. Alistair sheathed his sword, and went over to Hawk.

"It seems I owe you an apology. I was so sure you were the freak. But then, I'm only human."

Back in the library, the room became a bedlam as everyone talked at once, explaining and apologizing and generally relaxing. Holly fussed around Arthur, wrapping his broken hand in a cloth and trying to clean the blood from his face with a handkerchief soaked in wine. David kept squeezing Arthur's shoulder, and telling him incoherently how well he'd done. But finally Jamie confronted Hawk, and everyone else shut up so they could listen.

"I think you owe us some answers," said Jamie. "All right, we were wrong about you being the freak. I'm sorry, but you have been behaving very suspiciously. Who are you, really, and what are you doing here? And what the hell happened to your eye?"

"I can't tell you who I am," said Hawk flatly. "But I can tell you why I'm here. Isobel and I came here looking for someone."

"Who?"

Hawk turned and looked at David. "Do you want to tell them, or shall I?"

David shrugged, and met the MacNeil's gaze unflinchingly. "Sorry, Jamie, but I'm afraid I've rather let the side down. I'm a spy. I stumbled across a piece of information I knew Outremer would pay a hell of a lot for, and the temptation was just too great. I needed the money, you see. I owe a hell of a lot, what with one thing and another, much more than you ever knew about, and some of my creditors were becoming very insistent. There was even talk of debtors' prison. My Family had already made it clear they wouldn't be responsible for my debts any more, and without their backing the moneylenders wouldn't even see me.

"It wasn't difficult, making contact with Outremer. You'd be surprised how many agents they have here in the city. But in the end it all went wrong, and I ended up running for my life. So I came here, to hide out while I waited for my contact to show up. I had to come anyway, to see what Holly was going to get from the will. I was banking on her inheriting a fortune, to get me out of the hole I'd dug for myself. She'd have loaned me what I needed. Hell, you'd have given it to me outright; wouldn't you, Holly? You never could deny me anything."

"Why the hell didn't you ask me for the money?" said Jamie hotly. "I wouldn't have let you go under, for the sake of a miserable few thousand ducats."

"I couldn't ask you, or any of my friends," said David. "I didn't want you to know what a fool I'd made of myself.

I have my pride. It's all I've got left now. I won't give it up. I won't stand trial, either. Arthur, look after Holly.''

He turned and ran out the door, and into the corridor. Hawk and Fisher went after him. Hawk paused at the door to order everyone else to stay put in the library, and then he and Fisher charged down the corridor and up the stairs in pursuit of David Brook. They were both tired after their struggle with the freak, and David soon outdistanced them. They pressed on, following the sound of his feet on the stairs. They passed the second floor and the third, and still David led them on.

''Where the hell does he think he's going?'' panted Fisher. ''There's nowhere left now but the battlements, and once he's there, we've got him cornered.''

''Not necessarily,'' said Hawk. ''There's still one way down, if he wants to take it.''

They finally burst out into the morning air, and found David sitting on the edge of the far parapet wall, waiting for them. Fisher started forward, but Hawk put a restraining hand on her arm. The sunlight was almost painfully bright after the gloom of the third floor, and Hawk stood quietly a moment, letting his eye adjust. David sat patiently, his legs dangling over the long drop. He was smiling slightly.

''Come away from the edge,'' said Hawk finally. ''It's dangerous.''

''Look at the view,'' said David. ''Isn't it marvelous? It feels like you can see forever.''

''Is that why you dragged us all the way up here?'' said Fisher. ''To admire the view?''

David shrugged, and smiled. ''I won't ask you how I gave myself away. It doesn't matter. I was pretty much an amateur at the spying game, anyway. But I would like to know who you really are.''

''Hawk and Fisher, Captains in the city Guard,'' said Hawk. ''We're the ones who chased you through half of Haven last night.''

David raised an eyebrow. ''I'm impressed. I've heard some of the stories they tell about you two. Are they true?''

''Some of them,'' said Hawk.

"What did you do with the sorcerer Grimm?"

"We killed him," said Fisher.

"Good," said David. "The city probably smells better now he's gone. I wouldn't have dealt with him at all if my contact hadn't insisted."

"Who was your contact?" said Hawk.

David shrugged. "It was always someone different. They didn't trust me enough to let me see anyone important."

"What about the information?" said Fisher. "What was so important that so many people had to risk their lives because of it?"

David stared out across the sea. "The Monarch of Outremer is coming here, to Haven, to meet with our King and hammer out a Peace Treaty to put an end to the border clashes, before they start really getting out of hand. But there are those on both sides who would profit greatly from a war, people who don't want the peace talks to succeed. Knowing the exact date and time and place of those talks was therefore of very great value to those with an interest in sabotaging them. And I knew. I just happened to be in the wrong place at the wrong time, and nosy enough to look at a sheet of paper left lying carelessly on a desk. And that's how it all started. As simply as that."

"Come away from the edge," said Hawk. "You might fall."

"I'm not going back," said David. "If I were put on trial, it would disgrace my Family's name. I can't do that. I've been enough of a disappointment to them as it is. Besides, my friends would be found guilty by association, just for knowing me. And Holly would be hounded, ostracised, because she was close to me. I can't have that. I think Holly could be happy with Arthur. Don't you?"

"Yes," said Hawk. "He cares for her."

"Good," said David, and pushed himself out and away from the wall. He didn't scream, all the way down to the rocks at the bottom of the cliffs.

8

Saying Goodbye

The wards finally went down at ten o'clock the next morning. A subtle vibration came and went on the air, and the solid weight of Tower MacNeil seemed to settle itself more comfortably, and as suddenly and simply as that, it was over. Hawk ceremoniously opened the front door, and he and Fisher stepped out into the brisk morning air. It was a fine sunny morning, with only the cold nip of the wind to remind them of how close winter was. Gulls rode the wind on outstretched wings, crying and keening, and from far below came the endless crash of waves on the rocks.

Only Jamie and Robbie Brennan were there to say goodbye, and Hawk and Fisher were just as happy that way. It had been an uncomfortable time for all of them, waiting for the wards to go down. Hawk and Fisher might have saved the day, but their very presence was a reminder of things the MacNeils were eager to forget. The four of them stood together a moment, two within the Tower and two without, none of them sure what to say for the best. In the end, Jamie coughed awkwardly, and they all looked at him expectantly.

"You've done my Family a great service," he said firmly. "The freak is finally at rest, and the MacNeils are free of their Curse, if not their Shame. I wish you'd let me reward you in some way. Just saying thanks doesn't seem nearly enough.''

"Thanks are all we want," said Hawk. "We're just grateful you haven't insisted on knowing who we really are.''

"I have a strong feeling I should," said Jamie, trying not to stare at Hawk's closed right eye, "But I'm equally sure I wouldn't like the answer. You'd probably only lie, anyway.''

Hawk and Fisher grinned, and said nothing.

"I'm afraid we're all the send off you're going to get," said Brennan. "The others have all managed to be very busy just at the moment. Holly and Lord Arthur are comforting each other, as best they can. For the moment they both miss David too much to think of anything else, but I wouldn't be surprised if they ended up staying together. I think they'd be good for each other. Who knows? Maybe she'll even stop him drinking.''

Hawk smiled. "It's possible, I suppose. Stranger things have happened.''

"Aunt Katrina is upstairs packing," said Jamie. "I told her she was still welcome to stay as long as she wished, but it would appear she can't wait to leave. She says she doesn't feel safe here anymore. I can understand that. I've lived all my life in the Tower, and I don't feel the same about it now. It's as though an old and trusted friend had suddenly revealed a dark and violent side to his nature, something you'd never even suspected before. I'll probably get over it, but I don't think I'll ever really trust the Tower again.''

"Where's she going?" said Hawk.

Jamie shrugged. "Back to the city. I don't think she herself knows where she's going yet.''

"Maybe she'll go back to her husband," said Fisher.

"I hope not," said Brennan. "For his sake. I wouldn't wish Katrina on my worst enemy. At least not unless I was in a really nasty mood.''

"What about Alistair?" said Hawk. "He spent most of yesterday evening trying to avoid us.''

"He's around somewhere," said Jamie. "Hiding his

face. I think he still feels guilty about accusing you of being the freak. No doubt he'll turn up again, once you're safely gone.''

There was another pause as they ran out of polite, unimportant things to say.

''I'm sorry about David,'' said Hawk finally. ''He wasn't a bad sort. We would have taken him alive, if we could.''

''I know that,'' said Jamie. ''I've no doubt it happened just the way you described. David was many things, but he was never a coward. He knew there was only one thing he could do to protect his Family, and he did it. I don't know what I'm going to tell them. Some of the truth is bound to come out, eventually. I can't even bring his body home to them. The tides have already taken it out to sea. I still feel guilty about him, you know. I was his friend. I should have realized something was wrong. If I had, maybe I could have found a way to help him, before he got mixed up with the wrong people. . . .''

''Stop that,'' said Brennan firmly. ''If David had wanted you to know, he would have told you. He had enough opportunities. But his pride wouldn't let him. Or perhaps he just didn't want to drag his friends down with him. Whatever happened is his responsibility, no one else's. You're the MacNeil now, Jamie. You must learn not to worry about things that can't be changed.''

Jamie nodded slowly, but still looked unconvinced. Hawk decided this might be a good time to change the subject, and cleared his throat loudly. ''What about you, Robbie? What are you going to do with yourself, now that Duncan's left you such a sizeable windfall?''

Robbie grinned. ''Damned if I know, to be honest. But I might just do a little travelling. It's a long time since I was out in the world. There's bound to have been a lot of changes, and I think I'd like to see some of them while I still can. Not that I haven't been happy here, Jamie, but it's not the same with Duncan gone. I'll look back from time to time, see how you're getting on; sing you any new songs I've picked up.''

''Yes, of course,'' said Jamie. ''That would be nice.''

Brennan laughed. "You're not fooling anyone, Jamie. You never did appreciate my singing."

"It's an acquired taste," said Jamie solemnly. "And I've only been listening to you for about twenty years."

They all smiled genuinely, and Hawk put out his hand to Jamie. The MacNeil shook it firmly. There was a quick burst of handshaking all round, and Hawk led Fisher away, before the goodbyes could become awkward again. They set off down the trail that led to the city, and didn't look back.

"Well," said Hawk finally, "How did you like being one of the Quality, Isobel?"

Fisher snorted. "The food was good and the wines were splendid, but the company sucked and I hate their idea of fashion. The corset pinches me every time I breathe, having my hair piled up like this makes my head ache, and these shoes are killing me."

Hawk smiled. "Just be grateful we didn't have to mix with a dozen or more Families in High Society."

"I am grateful," said Fisher. "Believe me."

"I don't think we did too badly. We didn't hit anyone."

Fisher shook her head. "You don't have the right attitude for High Society, Hawk."

"Hark who's talking."

They laughed quietly together, and made their way back down towards Haven.

Alistair stood alone in the drawing room, looking up at the portrait of the Family Guardian hanging over the fireplace. The room was very quiet, the only sound the soft crackling of the fire. He knew he didn't have much time before the others would come looking for him, but still he hesitated, torn with indecision. It was such a long time since he'd last walked the corridors of the Tower. He hadn't realized he'd miss it so much.

He looked round the drawing room, deliberately not hurrying himself, taking in all the details. They'd made a lot of changes since his day. He didn't care for most of them, but then, fashions change. He walked slowly round the room, smelling the flowers and admiring the paintings and tapestries, and letting his fingers drift over the polished surfaces of the furniture. He couldn't stay. It was his home, but he couldn't stay. He didn't belong here anymore. The young girl Holly had begged for him to come, and so he had, but he wasn't needed anymore. The freak was dead at last, finally at peace.

He turned back to face the portrait again. It was time to go, before the others realized he wasn't really Alistair MacNeil after all. He wanted so much to stay, to walk in the real world, to see the sun rise and fall and feel the wind on his face . . . but he still had his penance to fulfill. The penance he'd taken on so many years ago, for the terrible things he'd done to his son, the freak.

The MacNeil Family Guardian held his head high and disappeared back into the portrait hanging over the fireplace, waiting to be called again, in time of need.

Whenever they might need him.